C.W.D.

"So are you here to apologize—or to replace me?" The bite was back in her tone with a vengeance.

"Certainly not to replace you, *yatāki mou*," he answered swiftly, his gaze wandering impertinently over her one-piece swimsuit. "Perhaps I came to see if you were obeying my instructions about not sunbathing topless."

"And perhaps you were surprised?" she shot back furiously. "Or even disappointed?"

His mouth twitched with curbed laughter. "Disappointed? Definitely not. When the time comes for me to enjoy the sight of your unclad body, it will give me the greatest pleasure to know it's a privilege not already extended to the community in general and my fellow countrymen in particular."

Angela Wells left the bustling world of media marketing and advertising to marry and start a family in a suburb of London. Writing started out as a hobby, and she uses backgrounds she knows well from her many travels for her books. Her ambitions, she says, in addition to writing many more romances, are to visit Australia, pilot a light aircraft and own a word processing machine.

Books by Angela Wells

HARLEQUIN ROMANCE
2790—SWEET POISON
2844—MOROCCAN MADNESS
2903—DESPERATE REMEDY
2921—FORTUNE'S FOOL

Still Temptation

Angela Wells

Harlequin Books

TORONTO • NEW YORK • LONDON
AMSTERDAM • PARIS • SYDNEY • HAMBURG
STOCKHOLM • ATHENS • TOKYO • MILAN

Original hardcover edition published in 1988
by Mills & Boon Limited

ISBN 0-373-03006-1

Harlequin Romance first edition September 1989

'For still temptation follows where thou art.'
Shakespeare *The Sonnets*

CHAPTER ONE

'DO YOU need help at all? Is someone meeting you, or are you trying to find a taxi?'

Verona started as the male voice sounded immediately behind her. Even before she turned, she knew the speaker would be Greek. The triple-aspirated 'h' in the word 'help' had betrayed what was otherwise a flawless accent.

'A taxi's just what I need!'

Relief shone clearly on her face as she relinquished her grip on her suitcase, turning to smile at her saviour. The smile wavered, then froze as she realised almost instantly that he wasn't, as she'd previously supposed, a cabbie plying for hire.

It wasn't his height, which judging from the way he towered over her must have been at least six feet two, or the clothes he wore. Certainly the latter were casual enough—light blue cotton trousers which even a cursory glance showed to be miraculously free of the crease-lines around knees and thigh which similar garments of equally close tailoring seemed to develop in other men; a white cotton shirt, short-sleeved, open-necked, the fine, almost transparent material seemed to lay like a second skin over a torso that embodied the qualities of grace and strength associated with an athlete.

Neither, she thought, momentarily entranced, was it the actual structure of his face. Heaven knew, there was no reason why a cab driver shouldn't share the characteristics of broad forehead, straight, arrogant nose, sensuously curved mouth and rounded, challenging chin

generally associated with the sculptures of Praxiteles—
they were, after all, in Crete! Even the dark head with
its thick, crisp covering of black hair and the equally
dark brows were no indication of trade or profession.

No, Verona decided after evaluating all the visual facts,
it was the way he was standing. That and the expression
on his smoothly tanned face, which made it quite clear
that, whatever he was doing at the airport, it had nothing
to do with driving a cab!

Quickly she reassessed her reaction, shocked to find
her heart tripping a light, fast rhythm beneath the navy
cotton of her sweater. Aware that she was finding his
presence oddly disruptive to clear thinking, she glanced
away from him, assuming a cool composure.

'Either there aren't any—or my eyes aren't as good as
they should be!' Shading her face, she stared out into
the sun-baked forecourt.

'There's nothing wrong with your eyes.'

It could have been a polite response, but the way the
words were drawled and the way his mouth curled with
appreciative pleasure left Verona in no doubt as to the
intended compliment.

Unwisely, she lifted her eyes to meet his gaze with the
full intention of quelling any further attempts at flirtation with a glance of icy indifference, only to find
herself blinking with shock on discovering that behind
the curtain of thick black lashes the deeply set eyes that
returned her appraisal with mocking intelligence were a
clear light blue, startlingly beautiful amid the darkness
of hair and skin that surrounded them.

Incredibly, Verona felt herself blush, a deep, warm
flow of colour rising from somewhere low in her body
and sweeping remorselessly up to her hairline. Desper-

ately she turned away, praying Katina would soon emerge from the crowd.

'Where are you staying?' Her companion's deep voice asked the question rhetorically, as he crouched down to examine the luggage tag on her case while she stood beside him helplessly, aware of the way the light cotton of his trousers stretched tautly over well-muscled thighs.

Conscious that she was behaving irrationally, Verona emitted a sigh of exasperation. She supposed she was more nervous than she'd realised about meeting Katina's brother, and the excitement of the flight, added to her friend's exuberance at returning home, plus the unaccustomed heat had made her less able to cope with simple matters like finding a taxi-cab at an international airport and dealing with disturbing members of the opposite sex!

'Iraklion itself, yes?' Her unwelcome companion had risen to his full height, apparently well content with what he'd ascertained. A quick, comprehensive glance from his startling eyes washed over her with a lazy impertinence, missing nothing, she fumed inwardly, from the fact that her hands were ringless to the beads of sweat that clung round her hairline, making her feel travel-stained and weary.

'Perhaps we shall have the pleasure of meeting again soon.' He bent his back, reaching out with a lean, tanned hand to grasp the handle of her case. 'Have you booked a hotel?'

'No, please. I...' Verona's hand seized on his arm in a forbidding gesture, withdrawing again quickly as she felt the warm muscle clench beneath her touch.

'No?' Dark brows lifted in mock surprise. 'I was only going to take your luggage to the taxi rank—not steal it.'

The air of injured innocence was beautifully done: intended to make her feel guilty. She'd never suspected he might be a thief—at least, she amended, not the kind of thief who stole suitcases from tourists! Her eyes narrowed slightly. But there were other kinds of thieves...good-looking young men who preyed on lonely female tourists, spending their weekends at airports seeing one conquest off before returning to find another on the next incoming plane. At the end of summer they'd acquired enough gold identity bracelets for their amorous services to see them through a comfortable, touristless winter!

A spark of mischief was born deep in Verona's heart. Sure now that she'd identified the handsome Greek as a professional playboy, she decided to have a little fun at his expense. Why not let him get her a taxi and listen in to the address she gave the driver? She repressed a smile, imagining the sort of reception he'd get if he tried to contact her at the Constanidou apartment. From what she'd heard of the formidable Andreas Constanidou, she didn't suppose he would look too kindly on the man who attempted to 'pick up' his young sister's companion!

'Of course you weren't. I realise that.' She met his wounded look with artless apology. Deliberately batting her eyelashes, she let her gaze travel with assumed admiration across his broad shoulders, drifting it downwards to cover the tight, lean span of his waist, not faltering as it traversed the line of narrow hip, long, muscled thigh and rigid calf, before returning to meet the speculative, almost brazen stare to which she was being subjected in return.

Verona gulped, conscious of a more powerful emanation of personality than she'd anticipated. Whoever he was, he was no amateur in his art, she accorded silently. Well, she'd certainly commandeered his entire attention; she might as well play the part out.

'You can't imagine how grateful I'd be if you could really find me a cab...' She pushed her dark blonde hair away from her face, deliberately smoothing her palm over her breast on its way down as if to remove non-existent creases, barely able to hide her amusement as his gaze followed its path, before returning to rest on her flushed cheeks.

For a few seconds he pinned her with his assessing stare and she read in the depths of his remarkable eyes the innate understanding of her provocative movement.

Then, instead of reaching for her case as she'd supposed he would, he lifted his arm. Subject to an unreasoning panic at the thought that he might touch her, Verona backed away, swivelling her head to look back into the terminal, her breath coming in a slow, sweet sigh of relief as she saw Katina struggling towards her, a suitcase in each hand.

On the point of going forward to help her, she paused, startled to see her friend dump both cases just clear of the exit doors, her face breaking into a smile of delight as she hurried forward empty-handed.

'I couldn't find a taxi...' she hastened to explain. 'I wasn't sure...'

The explanation died on her lips as, inexplicably, Katina ignored her, darting past to hold out her arms in a gesture of greeting towards the persistent Greek who stood behind her.

Strong hands clasped Katina's outstretched fingers, before Verona's bemused stare, as the younger girl was drawn into a warm embrace. Dark head lowered, the firm mouth brushed against Katina's cheek while the hard edge of sexual awareness in the light blue eyes that had pierced Verona's complacency was softened by affection.

'Andreas! Oh, Andreas, *mou*! You came to meet us after all!' Katina's voice rang out clearly in English.

Dear God! There had to be a mistake! Please let her have misheard! Verona felt her face blanch as she shook her head disbelievingly. She had to be suffering from jet lag or dehydration! How could this superb male animal, sleek and beautiful like a beast of prey, exuding an aura of latent sexuality that could turn the head of any female less well balanced and immune than herself—how could he possibly be Katina's stuffy, domineering brother?

For months now she'd had the image of Andreas Constanidou firmly fixed in her mind. He'd be an older version of Katina's cousin Petros—a short, thick-set, moustachioed young man whom she'd met occasionally when he'd come to meet Katina after evening classes. At thirty-two, Andreas's ideas would be no less reactionary than Petros's, who believed in the total superiority of man over woman. Hadn't Andreas's harsh line regarding Katina's return to Crete and the conspiracy he had evolved in her absence already proved this fact?

As for herself, she'd decided, he would treat her with a mixture of respect and coolness, as befitted an alien and unknown woman being introduced into his household through family misfortune to provide a necessary service.

Verona's nerves tingled alarmingly. *That* was the Andreas she'd expected. Not this paganly attractive, clean-shaven, wicked stranger whose approach to an unaccompanied young woman had certainly been open to misunderstanding!

'I got the meeting postponed, Kati.' He too spoke English, and now his eyes were narrowed, searching the still thronging crowds leaving the terminal. 'Your friend would think me a very bad host if I let two women attempt to cope with this rough and tumble alone.'

'And we're both very grateful.' Katina smiled up into his frowning face. 'But you don't have to look any further for Verona—you've already met her!' Suddenly aware of the silence around her when there should have been murmurs of assent, Katina stepped back from her brother's arm, which had remained carelessly across her shoulders. One glance at Verona's astonished face and she was pulling her forward, bringing her within a foot of the now glowering Greek, seemingly unaware of the tension that crackled between them like an unearthed charge of electricity.

'Verona,' she said formally, smiling brightly, her words destroying any last remaining hope the older girl had nursed. 'This is my brother—Andreas.'

Swallowing deeply, Verona composed her face into an expression of polite interest as Katina continued blithely, 'Andreas, meet my very best friend—Verona!'

A hand snaked out to grasp her chin, freezing the forced smile she had assumed as it trembled on her ripe mouth. Blue eyes like chips of arctic ice pierced through all her defences as a voice as keen and sterile as a scalpel sliced into her self-esteem.

'*You* are Verona Chatfield?' Andreas Constanidou demanded contemptuously. '*You?*'

It had not been an auspicious beginning to her stay in Crete.

Verona placed her empty cup on the polished onyx table-top in the sitting-room of Andreas Constanidou's Iraklion apartment and leant back in the luxuriously padded armchair.

Even weeks later, the memory of the short journey from the airport would be a blur of crowded streets and fast-moving traffic. Katina had chattered on happily, sitting next to her brother in the front of his white Mercedes, remarking on the sights and exclaiming excitedly at any changes she observed, seemingly oblivious of the atmosphere between her two companions in the car.

Probably, Verona thought wearily, Katina had put her own silence in the back seat down to the trauma of finding herself in a foreign country, and was blissfully unaware of the painful embarrassment she was experiencing.

If she'd had the slightest idea she'd ever set eyes on Andreas again she most certainly would not have pretended to respond to his philandering. Everything else apart, she had come to Crete intending to oppose what she saw as his high-handed and inhuman plans for Katina's future. Logic told her she hadn't ever stood much chance of changing his mind, but it had been imperative she should argue from a position of strength! Well, she determined grimly, she would just have to put the record straight as soon as she possibly could.

'I feel a lot better after that cup of tea,' she announced, giving her host a polite, impersonal smile.

Her words met with a curt nod. 'A great deal of my business is conducted with the British. I'm aware of the recuperative effect it has on them.' Andreas paused slightly before rising to his feet. 'Perhaps now you feel refreshed you'll come next door to my study. I think there are one or two things we need to discuss.'

'Yes, of course...' Verona started to reply before realising she'd been given an order, not a request, and

Katina's brother wasn't even waiting to hear her answer before striding out of the room.

So, all right, she thought defiantly, there'd been some sort of animal awareness between them at the airport. He hadn't known who she was and he'd tried to pick her up. Now he felt embarrassed and ashamed in case she told his sister that her respectable older brother was only human, after all! As it happened, she'd no intention of discussing him with Katina; on the other hand . . . it might not do any harm to let him squirm a little . . . His greeting to her had been decidedly less than courteous, hadn't it?

Composing her face into a mask of maidenly innocence, she left Katina about to go and unpack, and walked across the room into which Andreas had disappeared.

A quick glance round registered heavy rugs on the wooden floor, two deep swivel-based armchairs, a neat, modern desk and well-filled bookshelves.

'I take it you've recovered from your journey?' His tone was clipped and businesslike as she seated herself in the chair opposite him.

'Thank you, yes.' Verona paused before adding lightly, 'I think perhaps I was suffering from dehydration. I felt quite light-headed after we landed.'

It was the nearest she'd go to offering him an olive branch. A mere suggestion that she might not be prepared to recall his outrageous behaviour.

Eloquent eyebrows moved closer to his hairline. 'It's possible,' he conceded drily. 'Flying does have that effect, I understand. Normally it only occurs on long-distance flights, unless one is ill-advised enough to take over-advantage of the duty-free bar.'

There was no sign of remorse or humour on the Greek's hard face as, stung by his cynical comments, Verona rushed to defend herself.

'I shared half a bottle of white wine with Katina when we had lunch,' she flung back, her hazel eyes sparkling green with annoyance. 'Would you call that over-indulgent?'

'In your case it appears to have been very beneficial,' came the unperturbed response. 'Do I assume that's the reason thirty-odd years seem to have dropped from your age, and your hair has been restored to its original colour? Or,' he rose to his feet in one graceful movement to stand over her, gazing down into her bewildered face, 'am I to believe this rejuvenation is due to a face-lift and a bottle of peroxide?'

Verona gasped. If she could have found the strength to get up and march out of the room, she would have done just that! She hadn't come all this way to be insulted over her appearance! But the lean form of the Greek was threateningly close to her, and any movement on her part would only increase that proximity. Besides, she had Katina to consider.

'Well?' Andreas demanded remorselessly. 'I'm asking you what happened to the grey-haired, middle-aged widow whom I agreed to employ as a companion to my sister.'

'I'm sorry, but I've no idea at all what you're talking about!' Indignation brought a flush to Verona's cheeks and increased the rate of her heartbeat beneath her thin cotton top. 'I'm twenty-three, single and my hair is the same colour as when I was born.'

'So I see!' came the acid retort, infuriating her with its tone of cool scorn, and arousing in her a most untypical desire to wipe the sardonic sneer from his dark face with the palm of her hand.

Instead she took a long, shaky breath in an effort to retrieve her self-control. 'I think you owe me some kind of explanation,' she challenged coldly. 'I understood you were expecting me.'

'On the contrary, you're the one with the explaining to do...' Something in the way the sparkling light eyes surveyed her made a faint shiver run down Verona's back as he continued, 'When I asked my aunt for a description of you, I assumed she'd met you. As that obviously wasn't the case, I'm left with the conclusion that when she spoke to you on the phone to discuss the matter you deliberately gave her a physical description of yourself that you knew would meet with my approval.'

'Really?' What was it he'd said—'grey-haired, middle-aged widow'? Verona's resolve to stay calm evaporated with the speed of a Cretan river in the summer sun. 'If I'd known you had a fetish for elderly, faded widows I'd have circulated the job in the local old age pensioners' club instead of changing my own plans at such short notice to accommodate you!' she retorted furiously.

The gleam that brightened Andreas's eyes and the way he sucked in the corners of his mobile mouth didn't bode well for her, but Verona thrust her chin up defiantly. 'In any case, I was under the impression it was Katina's needs which were paramount—not yours!'

'And I decide what those needs are!'

She'd certainly added fuel to the anger simmering beneath the surface, Verona saw as he made an impatient gesture. 'As you no doubt know, I have a small villa on the coast outside Iraklion where my sister wishes to spend the summer. Apart from wishing to spare her the loneliness of being by herself, it so happens that a large in-

ternational hotel has recently opened at the resort.'
Compelling eyes stared down at her with calculated
impertinence. 'Unfortunately, as is usual in these
instances, it's attracted a number of young ladies from
the colder—climatically speaking, that is—European
countries, who seem to find the ardour and stamina of
our young Greek men attractive . . . if not irresistible.'

'Well, you should know . . .' she murmured with pointed
mockery.

The look he gave her would have withered her if she
hadn't been prepared for it.

'As a snowball effect,' he continued, ignoring her interruption, 'there's been a dramatic increase in the youths
who go down there from Iraklion and prowl the beaches
looking for a good time. Additionally, male tourists from
other countries aren't always aware of the respect with
which we treat our own women. Now!' His voice
sharpened, daring her to treat his attitude lightly. 'Do
you understand what I'm saying?'

'Yes, I believe so.' Verona determined to keep her
temper under control for Katina's sake, and certainly
she wasn't in doubt about his insinuations. 'On the basis
of a brief meeting between us, you've concluded that
I'm not a suitable companion for your sister.'

'Exactly!' he pronounced triumphantly. 'On that basis,
plus your concealing from my aunt the fact that you're
a young and beautiful woman. Frankly, I find your
motives in coming here questionable, to say the least.'

'Oh, really!' Too incensed to recognise the compliment within the accusation, Verona jumped to her feet
to slam her fist down on his desk. 'Well, let me tell you,
I didn't hide anything from anyone,' she stormed truthfully. 'At no time did your aunt ask me for a personal

description or say you wanted an elderly chaperon. She just confirmed the terms of your offer.'

In fact the poor woman had been too upset by her husband's having succumbed to chicken pox on what was virtually the eve of their planned return to Crete to indulge in any further conversation.

'So it was my aunt who lied to me?' His voice was icily composed, his eyebrows curving upward in cynical comment at her denial. 'To what purpose, do you suppose?'

'How should I know?' Verona expostulated. 'Why on earth didn't you ask Katina what I was like if it was so important to you? Or your cousin Petros, for that matter. We'd met on several occasions.'

'Because Petros wasn't available at the time, and my discussion with Katina had already ended.'

'Then...' Her voice tailed off. Aunt Irini must have asked Katina to describe her, and the Greek girl, aware of her brother's prejudices and his unspeakable plans for her future, but still desperate to return to her homeland, had given him a description she knew would be acceptable. Presumably she thought her imperious sibling would accept a *fait accompli*—and, equally clearly, her faith in Andreas's humanitarianism was misplaced.

Even to justify herself, she couldn't implicate Katina. Behind the patina of charm so effectively projected at the airport there lurked a cutting edge to 'big brother's' personality she wouldn't want to see honed on his vulnerable young sister.

'Yes?' he insisted quietly.

'Then it must have been a misunderstanding,' she finished weakly, furious with herself for the way she had mishandled the situation at the airport and precipitated this unwelcome storm. Righteous indignation had been the stance *she'd* been determined to assume in support of her young Greek friend when the crunch came. To find herself the accused instead of the accuser was mortifying. Since clearly any attempted intercession on Katina's behalf now would do more harm than good, the only dignified course left open to her was to cut her losses. At least, she thought philosophically, the first objective of returning Katina to her homeland had been achieved.

She lifted her slender shoulders in a negligent shrug. 'In any case, now you've made it quite clear I'm unwelcome, perhaps you'll arrange for a flight home for me?' She met his stern regard proudly, hopeful that the travellers' cheques she'd brought with her for personal expenses would cover the return fare.

It was with an effort that she kept the tremble of anger from her carefully modulated voice. This interview was a nightmare, hurtful and humiliating, and the sooner she escaped from Andreas Constanidou's unmerited wrath, the better for everyone concerned.

'That won't be necessary.' Andreas dismissed her request with a casual indifference. 'You may have misrepresented yourself to obtain a position of trust, but I've no intention of allowing you to shirk the duties you accepted.'

He allowed his eyes to range with unrestrained interest over her taut frame, lingering with a studied insolence on her seething breasts before passing over her protesting mouth, to focus finally on the stormy hazel depths of her eyes.

'I've little doubt you used my sister's affection and innocence as an excuse to enable you to come here solely for your own pleasure; but let me make it quite clear,

Verona Chatfield: you are not going to indulge your own desires at the expense of my pocket and my sister's happiness!'

Too shocked to formulate the words she needed to insult him as he deserved, Verona could only make inarticulate sounds of rage as her tormentor gave a brief, explosive laugh.

'You're shocked I speak so frankly? But I can assure you I haven't lived thirty-two years without learning a great deal about women—especially Northern Europeans with their so-called liberated viewpoints!'

'You know absolutely nothing about this one!' Defying his forbidding demeanour, she went to thrust her way past him, astounded when firm hands fastened on her shoulders, forcing her to a standstill.

'Then it'll be my pleasure and education to learn during the time you're a member of my household,' he told her without compromise.

'You think I'll stay here now? After your rudeness and absurd allegations?' Verona's eyes widened in honest amazement. The man was mad!

'Yes, I think so.' Stern-faced, he met her hostile challenge with calm assurance. 'You see, I'm prepared to make it worth your while to keep up the pretence that your concern for Katina's welfare is your only reason for being here, by paying you a bonus at the end of your stay.'

'You think you can *buy* my loyalty to your sister's interests?' Warm colour flooded Verona's cheeks as his disparaging remarks bit deep into her pride. 'What exactly do you expect to get for your money?'

'Your abstinence from erotic encounters during your visit.' The answer came back low and swift. A harsh edge of command sharpened his voice further. 'And that means you don't entertain male guests in my villa and you ignore the *kamaki* who prowl up and down the beach.'

'*Kamaki?*' Momentarily distracted, Verona queried the use of a meaningless name—'What are they—the Greek mafia?'—and had the pleasure of seeing Andreas's mouth tighten.

'*Kamaki*—it's the long trident you see on the fishing-boats. Here, when a man goes looking for a woman, we say he "makes *kamaki*"—you understand?'

'Yes, indeed.' A slow smile turned the corner of her lips. It was a neat way of describing what this impossible Greek had been attempting to do to her earlier that day at the airport.

As if guessing her thoughts, he pre-empted the words that were trembling on her tongue by sliding his gaze away from her face to dwell with calculated interest on the twin points of her rounded breasts.

'Neither shall I expect you to either embarrass my sister or offend my neighbours by sunbathing without the top of your bikini on the public beaches as so many of your countrywomen do.'

'I'm actually allowed to wear a *bikini*?' Verona's sarcasm was knife-edged as she shot her eyebrows skyward in dramatic surprise, feeling a warm glow of satisfaction as his brow furrowed at the tartness of her retort. She might have been wrong about his looks, but not about his being reactionary!

'Don't sharpen your claws on me, *yatáki*,' he admonished softly, a frown creasing his broad forehead. 'I know what's best for my sister, and by *Theo*, you won't be allowed to spoil the coming weeks for her.'

'Indeed I shan't,' she agreed tartly. 'Since I shan't be here to do so!'

'So...' Once more he barred her passage as she would have moved. 'You admit it at last. You care nothing for Katina!'

'Oh, I care for her.' With a tremendous effort Verona restrained herself from slapping the smugly complacent face in front of her. 'It's *you* I don't care for, with your outdated ideas and arrant discourtesy. Believe me, my heart weeps for Katina, having to spend the summer alone with you!'

'Then you can save your tears—because she'll be travelling back to England with you.'

Eyes as bright as glaciers beneath an arctic sky demolished any hope that he might not be serious. Verona made no attempt to hide the blazing scorn that lent green sparks to her long-lashed eyes. Just as she'd thought! Andreas Constanidou had no intention of being lumbered with his seventeen-year-old-sister—that was starkly obvious.

'You'd do that to her? You'd really send her back to England when you must know how homesick she's been for the past few months?' Contempt laced her tone.

'Not me—you.' His smile was triumphant as Verona realised with a sinking feeling that she'd been trapped. Although why he should want her to stay after everything he'd said was a mystery.

He gave a slight shrug of his powerful shoulders, divining her puzzlement.

'You're not what I was led to believe, but the fact remains that business prevents me from being with Katina all the time, and I'm not prepared to leave her for long periods by herself. I don't know what she's told you about the circumstances that resulted in her spending a year in England, but the fact is that Katina was alone with our mother when she suffered a fatal stroke. It was very sudden, totally unexpected, and the effect on Kati was traumatic.' He paused thoughtfully. 'She is, I think, fully recovered, but I'm not prepared to chance her suffering a relapse into depression. She needs a companion, someone she likes and trusts.' A rueful twist of his lips conveyed Andreas's own opinion as he continued, 'Apart from our Aunt Irini, it seems you are the only other person who has become close to her. My aunt assures me Katina regards you as a very dear friend.' Again he paused, considering Verona's tight-lipped pale face with a steady appraisal. 'For Katina's sake, I should like her to continue to do so.'

His eyes narrowed, observing the hard set of her features which betrayed her mental conflict. 'If you return to England it will be impossible to find a replacement for you. So I'll have no option but to send her back immediately to the care of Yorgos and Irini.'

It wasn't an idle threat. Verona gritted her teeth in frustration. How could she possibly subject her friend to the disappointment of such a decision? Besides, from everything Katina had confided in her over the previous months, she understood that the fifteen-year age gap between brother and sister had already resulted in their relationship's being less close than it might ideally have been. Verona had been hoping a new and stronger link would be forged between them during the next few weeks. A link that would make Andreas more amenable to reason when it came to Katina's future.

'Very well,' she agreed tautly. 'For Kati's sake, I'll stay.'

'Excellent!' For the first time since she'd entered the room his personable face relaxed into a smile. The kind of smile a triumphant gladiator might have worn, thought Verona sourly, her whole body shaking with scarcely concealed fury as his glance lingered on her face. 'I take it we understand each other?'

Her lips moved in a wry grimace of distaste. 'I most certainly understand *you*, Mr Constanidou.' She endowed the words with scorn and saw the smile fade from his lean face.

'I intended you should. I also intend Katina shall not be disturbed by any hint of animosity between the two of us,' he instructed tightly.

'But naturally,' Verona agreed, tossing him a false smile. 'I'm an excellent actress!'

She could have bitten her tongue as she received a knowing grin for her pains.

'Indeed—I've enjoyed your performance of outraged dignity very much. At times I almost believed it.'

'Why, you . . .' Her control untethered at last, Verona lifted her arm to strike his mocking face, giving a sharp cry as he swung up his own hand, grabbing her wrist and using it to pull her towards him until she stood so close she could feel the warmth from his lean, hard body enveloping her.

'Listen to me, *yatáki mou*.' His mouth was so close, she could feel his warm, sweet breath against her cheek. 'You will call me by my given name—Andreas—but in all other ways when we're not alone you will treat me with respect. And when the time comes for you to leave, provided you've abided by my rules, I'll see you well rewarded. Understood?'

She hated him so much at that moment that she would have agreed to anything just to escape the threat his unbridled chauvinistic masculinity posed her.

'Understood!' she hissed between her teeth, rubbing the wrist he'd held as he freed her.

Damn the man! His actions had all the megalomaniac splendour of the ancient gods! And as for reward...she'd pay back every *drachma* he spent on her at the first opportunity.

'And you can call me Verona,' she retorted swiftly, not to be cowed by his dictatorial attitude, her tone acid with dislike. 'Not *yatáki mou*—whatever that means.'

'Yatáki?' He looked amused. 'It means a small cat.'

'A kitten?' She looked at him in disbelief. 'As in soft and warm and cuddly?' she queried sardonically.

He shook his head, blue eyes sparkling with a mocking superiority.

'You haven't seen our Greek cats yet, have you? They're slender and predatory, with long, slanting eyes and more than their fair share of feline cunning—*yatáki mou.*'

Verona smiled sweetly at his provocation. 'Thank you at least for not adding "big ears and whiskers". Do I have your permission to go now?'

She'd meant the question to sound sarcastic, but Andreas merely nodded as if it was natural she should ask his permission to leave the room. As he glanced down at his watch, his whole attitude suddenly changed.

'I thought we'd have dinner out tonight in Iraklion, and then, if you don't mind sharing a room with Katina for one night, I'll drive you both down to the villa in the morning.'

'Whatever pleases you.' She shrugged graceful shoulders, and if he recognised the edge to her reply he ignored it. 'Oh ... and Andreas ...' On the threshold of the room she paused.

An arched eyebrow acknowledged the use of his name and told her she had all his attention.

'Your command of English is remarkable,' she informed him in dulcet tones. 'Quite, quite outstanding!'

'Thank you.'

Did she fancy a smirk of self-satisfaction at her gentle compliment?

'There's just one thing...' She stood poised to leave the room and dared to laugh at him. 'I don't know about Crete, but in England we don't have "erotic encounters". We have "love affairs".'

The look she gave him was beautifully patronising, and perfect to accompany what should have been the last word. But Andreas Constanidou was too fast for her. Three quick strides brought him to her side as a strong arm curled round her waist, while a firm hand imprisoned her proudly defiant chin.

'And I don't know about England,' he told her with a soft but deadly emphasis as he stared down into her angry eyes. 'But here in Crete, Verona—*you* don't have either!'

CHAPTER TWO

THE WHITE Mercedes was moving at a steady hundred kilometres per hour over the coastal road in a westerly direction. From her position in the front passenger seat, Verona stared out at the oleander-lined highway.

Andreas drove well, she had to concede. It was the only thing she'd allow in his favour. His absurd implication that she was on a man-hunting expedition and in pursuing that purpose might neglect his sister would have been ludicrous if it hadn't been so insulting!

The only male head she'd like to win would be Andreas's own so she could serve it on a plate, glazed with redcurrant jelly and with an orange in its mouth. A highly suitable way of presenting the head of a chauvinist swine, she congratulated herself with grim humour.

The truth was, her most rewarding relationships with the male sex had been cerebral rather than physical. She'd achieved in her small circle of acquaintances what modern woman officially strove for—appreciation for her mental capacity and academic prowess rather than her body. It was a state of affairs with which she was well satisfied, she congratulated herself.

After all, emotional involvement blurred observation, distorting the truth. To date, her life had been too full, firstly with the excitement of increasing her knowledge and bringing her university education to a satisfactory conclusion, and later trying to use her hard-won

28

qualifications to their best purpose, for her to have considered forming an intimate relationship with a man.

Besides, she admitted, watching the grey ribbon of road being eaten beneath the Mercedes's wheels, in all honesty she'd never met a man who'd invoked in her any stronger feeling than that of friendship.

She smiled reminiscently, recalling her mother's advice before the latter had left to take up a new life in the States with her second husband.

'Don't make the same mistake I did,' Rosalie Chatfield had exhorted her earnestly. 'I married your father because he was a junior partner in my own father's company. We were thrown together socially and somehow it became expected of us. We even began to believe we loved each other—but after you were born we grew apart.' She'd shaken her head sadly. 'It wasn't anyone's fault in particular. Your father was a good man—but I needed more than that...and he wanted more from me than I was able to give.' She had paused, and there had been tears in her eyes as she'd looked at her daughter. 'Of course, when he died so young, I was grieved and angry, but even then I knew that if death hadn't separated us the divorce courts would have.'

Verona sighed pensively. Her mother was a darling, who since her early widowhood had managed magnificently, bringing up her only daughter and holding down an exciting and demanding job in advertising. Verona could think of no one who'd deserved happiness more, and when Rosalie had agreed to marry the American account director at the agency eighteen months ago and return to Los Angeles with him she'd been delighted.

She'd also been adamant in refusing their offer of a home for her with them in the States. She wanted to be free and independent and allow her mother the unhampered joy she so thoroughly deserved. In many ways the old cliché applied—the two of them had been more like sisters than mother and daughter, and Verona had begun to wonder recently if she too had it in her to fall in love with the joyous abandon that had characterised Rosalie's successful affair.

If only her job in the personnel department of Consolidated Industries hadn't turned out to be so soul-destroyingly boring, she mused now, that in a moment of frustration she'd handed in her notice—and in consequence been free to accept Katina's tearful pleading that she accompany her to Crete for two months, or if Uncle Yorgos hadn't succumbed to chicken pox...she might even now be searching for a proper job instead of sitting next to this archetypal Greek who knew nothing and cared even less about her qualifications or her ethics, yet was still prepared to pass judgement on her!

She turned her blonde head to glower at Andreas from beneath lowered lashes. It had gone against the grain to agree to his offer of payment for what, at the time, had promised to be an idyllic interlude. On the other hand, two months was a long time away from a shrinking job market. So, reluctantly, she'd agreed to accept reimbursement for her services—which was a pity, because it put her under an obligation to him!

Who would have thought when, barely a year ago, she'd been a temporary lecturer in sociology at the evening college where Katina had been studying English, that their casual meeting in the college canteen would have blossomed into a deep friendship which had made it impossible to turn down the teenager's urgent plea for help?

'Say you'll come back with me,' Kati had sobbed over

the telephone late one evening. 'Please, Verona! Andreas won't let me go home unless I have someone to stay with me.'

'How can I, Kati?' Even now, Verona could remember her initial response. 'There are so many other things I must do...'

'Andreas won't let me go by myself...' The young voice had been reed-like and broken. 'And, Verona, there's something else. Aunt Irini says that Andreas has found a husband for me. She wasn't supposed to say anything but it slipped out...and—and I'm so miserable I don't know what to do...'

Her eyes intent on the strong profile of the Greek beside her, Verona had no doubt in her mind as to what *she* would have said and done if she'd been Katina, but then, she recognised grimly, *she* hadn't been brought up in a patriarchal society under the harsh authority of a brother many years her senior. Marriage, indeed! And to a stranger! Apparently, after dropping her bombshell Aunt Irini had clammed up, leaving her niece with the impression that she'd been matched with some business associate of her brother's, and that it was her duty to comply with Andreas's wishes.

The news had swayed Verona's decision. Even if she hadn't filed her own mother's advice away in her memory, she would have found it impossible to accept the young Greek girl's fate without attempting to intercede on her behalf. At least, that had been her plan when she'd agreed to accompany Katina, although she hadn't said as much to her friend, sensing the younger girl's abject fear of a family row. No, she'd decided to bide her time until the right occasion presented itself before privately accosting Andreas on the subject.

It had never been going to be easy. Now, she thought with a burning frustration, it would be practically impossible to broach the matter with any hope of making him more amenable to reason! But that wouldn't stop her trying when the opportunity arose, as surely it soon must?

'You'll see this part of the north coast has escaped much of the tourist development that's occurred to the east of the city. Aghia Renagia itself is practically unspoiled.' As if guessing he was the subject of her thoughts, Andreas broke the silence, addressing his remarks to Verona's quickly averted profile.

'Except for the international hotel,' she murmured drily, remembering his earlier denigration.

'Except for that—yes,' he agreed cordially. 'Although *you* may find some of the attractions it offers pleasurable.'

The goad was slight, but unmistakable. Instantly Verona rose to it.

'I was under the impression they'd been barred to me.'

Her waspish tone earned her a flashed look. 'Not all of them,' Andreas disagreed politely. 'I had in mind the English bookshop and the hairdressers.'

Verona summoned up a cool smile. On the point of saying truthfully that she could manage to wash and set her own hair without professional help, she changed tactics. 'You mean, I'll need the latter when my grey hairs start to show through?' she answered tartly, and saw his mouth twitch at the corners.

'You're very determined to see I don't forget your misdeeds. You remind me of a naughty child who feels she deserves more than a scolding before she can be forgiven. What's the matter, Verona? Do you feel justice would have been better served if you'd been slapped?'

Warm blood suffusing her cheeks, Verona reacted to his patronising tone. 'As far as I'm concerned, the question of forgiveness has never arisen,' she shot back heatedly. 'I told you . . .'

'What on earth are you two talking about?' Katina's puzzled voice interrupted from the back seat. 'Why should Verona want to be slapped, and whatever do you mean about your hair, Verona? There's never been a streak of grey in it!'

'I think we're all aware of that fact!' Andreas's reply quivered with hidden laughter. 'And as for Verona being slapped—that's just a private joke arising from our little talk yesterday.' He paused before adding softly, 'I'm sure it's quite the last thing she wants.'

The mortifying colour on her face deepened at his subtle insinuation. Just let him try to manhandle her and she'd knee him where it hurt most, she determined with untypical vindictiveness—that would take the supercilious smile from his face. An inner caution warned her that she'd better leave herself plenty of space to run if she was driven to revenge of that nature. Andreas Constanidou wasn't the kind of man to suffer abuse without retaliation. She hadn't needed a university education to divine that!

Surprised at the power of her reaction and her discovery of an aggression she'd never suspected she possessed, Verona glanced obliquely at the man at her side. Set aside the good looks and what was left to hint at his character? Not dissipated enough to be a playboy, not unmarked enough to be a layabout: laughter lines around the eyes and mouth hinted at a sense of humour—although that hadn't been much in evidence to date! A womaniser? Oh, but definitely. Unmarried at thirty-two he might be, but that didn't mean he'd forsworn the joys of female companionship. If she'd ever had doubts about *that*, yesterday's volatile encounter at the airport would have crushed them.

Katina loved him; but that love was enhanced by awe. Understandable because, as her friend had confided in her, after her father had died Andreas had taken over her life. It was natural his young sister should look at him and see a man worthy of admiration. For Verona herself, it was quite different. All she could see when she looked at his classic profile was a stubborn, reactionary, chauvinistic, hypocritical bigot!

'There it is!'

Alerted by Katina's cry, Verona tore her thoughts away from the knotty problem Andreas's hostility posed her to gaze with interest as the car swung down the winding incline towards Renagia.

The small village clustered round the curve of white sand lay in the distance beneath them. It was picture-postcard beautiful—aquamarine water stretching out towards a deeper hue merging into the far horizon. At the sight of it Verona's natural optimism rose to the surface. With the brute at her side returned to Iraklion, she might yet be able to relax and enjoy Katina's company without interference.

The villa was about two hundred metres from the beach, built into the rising ground where it began to merge into the foothills. Built in typical Cretan style, its white-painted walls were relieved from severity by the arched balcony which surrounded the first floor and from which cascades of bright flowers tumbled earth-wards towards the ground-floor garage.

Downstairs, a large sitting-room and spacious kitchen were bisected by an open-tread staircase leading to two bedrooms—one double-bedded, the other holding two single beds, each room sharing a well-equipped bathroom. Eagerly Verona surveyed her surroundings, the floors of polished imitation marble, the elegantly modern furniture and the breathtaking views from the wide balcony.

'Does it come up to your expectations?'

Having been aware of Andreas watching her closely as Katina proudly escorted her round, she was prepared for the question.

'I didn't know what to expect—but it's quite lovely,' she answered honestly, hesitantly touching the base of the nearest bed before turning astonished eyes to his watchful face. 'The beds are made of concrete?'

'They're built when the house is,' Andreas explained, smiling at her horrified expression. 'Only the surround, though; then wooden slats are put in to form a base for a sprung mattress.'

'Very practical,' she approved, relief showing on her face.

'Unless you're a honeymoon couple under the mistaken belief that you're going to be able to push them together.' His lingering smile mocked her.

'I see you took that point into consideration when you had the other bedroom built!' The words escaped before Verona had judged their advisability.

'Naturally,' Andreas agreed silkily. 'I try to take most facts into consideration before I make a decision. Only rarely do I miscalculate...' He allowed his cool gaze to wander over her meaningfully. 'Fortunately there are usually means of rectifying any small error of judgement I may make.'

'I'm glad to hear you only make *small* errors. You must find that very comforting.'

Broad shoulders shrugged indolently at the retort. 'Everything is comparative, but yes, I've never lost control of any situation yet.'

'How interesting!' Verona tossed him a superficial smile. Really, this man was impossible. He was going out of his way to needle her, confident he'd bought her obedience. Dear God, how she was looking forward to seeing his face at the end of her stay when she told him what he could do with his 'bonus'.

'We have a proverb in England that warns us there is a first time for everything,' she informed him sweetly.

'Fascinating,' came the answering drawl, and suddenly the room was too small for both of them. Verona took a faltering step backwards, feeling as if she was being swamped by the powerful presence of the tall, grimly smiling Greek. 'I have a feeling I may have to remind *you* about that one day soon...'

'Verona...?' Katina's voice wafted in from the other room, breaking the growing atmosphere between them. 'Which room do you want?'

Before Verona could compose herself to reply, let alone think about making a decision, Andreas's cool voice answered on her behalf. 'Oh, Verona's quite happy where she is now, Kati. You keep the double bed.'

There was a wicked provocation in the glinting awareness of his remarkable eyes as Andreas lowered his voice to a husky whisper for her ears alone. 'There aren't going to be any trial honeymoons this trip, Verona—remember?'

She drew an unsteady breath, forgoing any thought of caution, infuriated by his sly insinuation. 'You amaze me, Andreas,' she told him coldly. 'If you're under the impression it's only possible to make love in a double bed, you're more old-fashioned than even I would have credited.'

She watched, choking with frustration, as, impervious to her attack, he twisted his mouth in amusement. Her body taut with annoyance at her failure to sting him, she looked away, unable to meet the malicious glint in his expression.

'On the contrary, I'm sure it's possible to make love on a four-inch beam,' he riposted gently, 'if the need is that imperative; but it would undoubtedly be less comfortable.'

'Really?' She refused to be nettled. 'Unfortunately the school I went to was single sex, so we didn't have the opportunity for that kind of experiment in the gymnasium.' Four-inch beam, indeed! The very idea was preposterous. 'While you, no doubt...'

She stopped abruptly, furious to feel a rising warmth overcoming her whole body. She must have been mad to engage in this kind of repartee with Andreas. It was serving no useful purpose and only giving him the chance to provoke her further.

'While I... what?' he encouraged her softly.

Fortunately the need for an answer was eliminated by Katina's sudden appearance in the room via the adjoining bathroom.

'Whatever are you two talking about in here?' Her affectionate glance passed between them, resting on her brother. 'If I'm to have the other room, can you bring my luggage across, please, Andreas?'

'Of course.' He lifted the two suitcases and followed her. 'I was just telling Verona I hoped you'd both have a quiet and restful stay here, and assuring her I shall be in touch to see there aren't any problems.'

'Whatever problems could there be?' Katina smiled up at him, her large brown eyes brimming with innocence. 'We've got everything here we could possibly want!'

'My point exactly.' His voice floated across the empty room. 'Oh, and I shall need to see your passport, Verona. Bring it down to me, please, while I turn the car around.' Re-entering the room, he walked past her without so much as a glance in her direction.

'Yes, sir!' she muttered under her breath. 'At once, sir!' It wouldn't have hurt him to wait the few seconds she needed to get the document from her hand-luggage. The peremptory command was just another way of demonstrating that he expected unquestioned obedience from her, damn him!

It must be one of the quirks of nature, she thought, angrily turning out the contents of her bag, that the gentle, shy Katina should spring from the same bloodline as her dominating, opinionated brother—or, she sighed inwardly as she found the passport, could it just be another example of conditioning from babyhood—the 'male superiority' myth that made Andreas Constanidou so intractable?

With cool determination she took her time before descending to ground level, where she found Andreas waiting for her in the sitting-room. Extending the stiff-covered document to him with mute indifference, she turned to go.

'Just a minute...'

'Yes?' she asked defensively, suspecting some further instruction to limit her activities. Her patience was being sorely tried, and she was in no mood to hide the churlishness of her feelings. Incredibly, her stony stare was met with a gentle twist of his lips as light eyes, half veiled by the sweep of dark lashes, regarded her with the magnetic warmth she'd last encountered at the airport.

Totally flummoxed by this sudden change of approach, Verona hesitated, watching with a wary incomprehension as he moved towards her.

'I forgot to give you something.'

The simple statement only partly calmed the rising panic that unaccountably tingled a message of warning through her tense body. The keys! He must mean the keys to the villa.

'Yes?' She stumbled the word out, conscious that his eyes were disquietingly intent, and unwillingly aware of how disturbingly attractive he was when he wasn't being deliberately objectionable. Forced to recognise that she was in the presence of a vibrant masculine magnetism, Verona could only be scared by the power it seemed to exert over her.

Unsuccessfully she tried to drag her gaze from the unmistakable invitation in his eyes: too blinded by their brilliance to heed the danger, she stood transfixed like a rabbit hypnotised by the approaching headlights of a car, while her mouth grew dry and the blood thundered in her ears.

Andreas's arms met with no resistance as he drew her slowly up against him, but he felt the sudden tension which made her back rigid as his hands encompassed her waist to complete the snare.

Dazed hazel eyes rose beseechingly, half afraid of what they might read on the lean face so close to them. Verona's soft mouth opened in formal protest, only to be deprived of the power of sound as Andreas lowered his head, moving his warm mouth in a slow caress to silence her.

Like velvet, his lips nuzzled the hot, dry silk of her own which tingled beneath them. With a slow, indolent pressure he drove all thoughts of resistance from her mind.

She couldn't cope. Like a computer receiving conflicting data, she just couldn't function, Verona thought wildly. She detested this man with good reason, and he'd made no secret of the fact that he despised her. But the feedback from her body was telling her something quite different. It spoke of a warm male body, fragrant and demanding; a strong, sweet, masculine mouth, teasing and considerate.

Every nerve in her body sang out in delight. Every pore of her skin defied her intelligence and expanded in pleasure, as a shattering realisation pierced her understanding. Feeling her body change, soften, transmute, she knew that for the first time in her life she was being kissed by a man who could override all logical objections and shake the foundations of her rational control!

Alarmed and shocked at her own response to a virtual stranger, she made no movement to protest when his firm hands unloosened her tremulous fingers and Andreas stood clasping her wrists, staring down at her with liquidly beautiful eyes as she strove to regain mastery over her besieged emotions.

'Well, *yatáki mou*...?' His eyes glittered with a fierce blue fire, the husky tone of his voice thickening and deepening the sound so it was little louder than a growl between the laboured breaths that rhythmically swelled his broad chest. 'I see it's a good job I remembered...'

Conscious of the irregular movements of his thumb against her wrists, her gaze pinned to the flexing muscles beneath his cleanly sculpted cheekbones, Verona shook her head uncomprehendingly.

'It's going to mean a long time for you without the consolation of male company if you mean to honour our agreement.' He gave a harshly humourless laugh. 'That was just something to keep the memory alive for you in the meantime.'

A fierce spurt of anger flared deep down inside her as Verona's eyes widened with shock. How dared he choose this way to humiliate her, to reinforce his instructions in a hurtful and demeaning way as if she were some mischievous teenager hell-bent on involving his sister in some licentious scandal?

Bitter shame curled through her as the need to strike back at his oversized ego became a demanding force.

'*That* was something to remember!' Her low voice quivered with the weight of her anger. 'Is *that* the best you can do? Let me tell you, *that* was about as memorable as the kiss the local council candidate gave me when I was four years old!' She was actually shaking with a mixture of emotions as she told the lie, unable to move from the spot where her pale face accused him, to seek the sanctuary instinct told her she needed.

'And which you still recall after nineteen years?' Deceptively soft, his reply might have calmed her if she hadn't been too aware of the calculating glint behind his lash-shielded gaze. 'Well, I'm sure I can surpass your political friend...'

Using her arm as a lever, Andreas pulled her further into the room, backing against one of the armchairs, sinking down into its upholstered depths and pulling her down on top of him.

She'd taunted him with her supposed experience and now he was intent on calling her bluff. Panic-stricken, Verona fought wildly as he half turned, pinning her between his body and the angle of the chair where arm met back. His mouth lacked its former tenderness as it found hers, forcing her lips apart by sheer tenacity of purpose to receive his deep caresses, while one hand stroked her honey-blonde hair away from her flushed cheek.

Arching her back, Verona tried desperately to evade the silky tenacity of his warm mouth, sighing in despair when it left her throbbing lips of its own accord to follow the line of her jaw and travel down the exposed pale curve of her throat.

Too conscious of the warmth of his body beneath the light fabric of his clothes, the delicious, evocative scent of his hair and skin and his quickened breathing, not to realise that behind his aggressiveness Andreas was responding to the feel of her female body beneath him in a very masculine way, Verona gathered all her remaining strength to free herself.

This time, his point made to his satisfaction, Andreas made no attempt to restrain her. Pushing himself away, he regained his feet, standing looking down at her dishevelled, distraught appearance, his expression unreadable.

Her breath sawing rapidly between her plundered lips, her throat still sensitive to the moist caresses so ardently planted upon it, Verona struggled to find the words she wanted to flay him with verbal abuse in exchange for the casual, uninvited intimacy he'd inflicted on her.

Eyes coloured with mocking amusement watched her abortive conflict with every sign of satisfaction.

'That's something else you must remember,' he told her calmly. 'We Greeks have been laying down and accepting challenges from the beginning of time. That's how the Olympic Games started.'

'What a pity they don't include a class for the type of games *you* enjoy playing!' At last she'd found her voice, as furious with herself as she was with her overbearing tormentor. Despite the fact that he'd been showing his contempt, she'd actually found his physical nearness far from repulsive, and was horrified by the implications of the discovery.

'I'm not playing games, *yatáki mou.*' His disconcerting gaze lost its humour, leaving him grim-eyed and stern. 'Put one foot wrong, expose Katina to unwelcome or unsuitable contacts, and you'll be on your way back to England before you have time to take a second breath—and without any financial compensation to soften the blow.'

Studiously Verona forced herself to ignore both his threat and the hand he offered to help her rise from the chair. If it hadn't been for Katina she would leave immediately! Talk about unwelcome contacts! They didn't come much more unwelcome than Katina's unpleasant brother!

'Verona!'

She'd stormed past him, and now she paused on the bottom stair, turning stiffly at the imperative use of her name. 'I thought you'd already had the last word?'

She addressed her remark somewhere above his head, refusing to be trapped into meeting the gaze which both fascinated and repelled her.

'Not quite,' came the quiet response. 'I have to return to Iraklion now, but I'll be back to see how you're enjoying your holiday.'

Verona accorded him a brief nod of her golden head in tacit acknowledgement. It could have been the parting remark of a considerate host.

Only they both knew it wasn't.

CHAPTER THREE

'I THOUGHT Andreas would have come over to see us before now,' Katina said pensively, as she helped herself to the black cherry conserve. 'I guess he must be very busy. Probably putting off that meeting to come to the airport caused him extra work.'

'Mmm.' Verona made a non-committal reply. She, too, had expected an early visit, for reasons she had not divulged to her friend!

Ten days had passed since her last abrasive meeting with Katina's brother, and she'd enjoyed every single one of them. Both girls had adapted themselves easily to the unhurried pattern of life around them, sunbathing and swimming, taking a couple of hours' siesta in the hottest part of the day and spending the evenings having late dinner on the terrace, watching the fishing fleet go out while the moon rose over the point and the breeze from the sea wafted the sound of bouzouki music from the tavernas.

They'd been idyllic days, during which Verona's fair skin had acquired a pale golden tan and her hair, bleached by sun and sea, had developed paler blonde highlights. She looked good and felt marvellous.

The small resort of Aghia Renagia was paradise and, as far as she was concerned, the longer the serpent stayed away in Iraklion, the better!

'You don't like Andreas.'

Katina's disappointment was evident in the flat tone of her statement.

Oh, dear. Verona cast her friend a quick glance. Her face must have shown the feelings she tried not to betray in her voice, and now the other girl was hurt by her reaction to a member of her family.

She shrugged her shoulders, taking a casual sip of her breakfast coffee. 'I don't like the idea of his choosing a husband for you, Kati.' For the first time since arriving in Crete she mentioned the subject that must surely be occupying Katina's thoughts.

The Greek girl gave a rueful smile. 'Neither did I when Aunt Irini first mentioned it. It was a bit of a shock, but I've had time now to get used to it.' She looked thoughtful. 'I suppose, now I'm not needed at home, I could find myself a job. In fact, that's what I intended to do once I got back. The other alternative would have been to act as housekeeper for Andreas, but he's always looked after himself, and I imagine his life is very well ordered and he wouldn't want me interfering in it.'

Verona thought the same, although probably not for the same reasons as her friend. She felt her mouth tighten disapprovingly as Katina went on speaking.

'But all I've ever really wanted to do was to get married and raise my own family, love them and look after them, watch them grow up and be happy...' She gave a slight shrug of her slim shoulders. 'It might not be so bad, after all. Andreas is bound to choose someone he likes and trusts.'

'And you'll accept him—just like that?' Verona asked in astonishment. 'Surely you can tell both Andreas and his candidate to go to blazes? No one can force you into marrying a man you don't know!' But that wasn't Katina's style, and Andreas must know that as well as she, Verona, did!

'I owe it to Andreas to please him in this matter.' Katina stared down at her hands. 'It's like Aunt Irini told me. It's my duty. The least I can do to repay him for everything he's done for me.'

'I can't really accept that, Kati,' Verona said gently. 'It's fine feeling gratitude and I can understand your wanting to please him, but not in something as important as marriage. I mean, your whole future's at stake after all; you're not eighteen yet.'

'But I soon will be.' Katina sounded surprised. 'And that's not at all young for marriage—not for a Greek girl whose future husband can afford to get married or whose family will help them set up home.'

'Well, yes,' Verona conceded the point on age. After all, the age of consent in England was sixteen. But the matter of choice was something she couldn't accept. 'But from what your Aunt Irini let slip, you think this man Andreas has in mind is someone he knows through business. Surely it looks as if he has only his own interests at heart—not yours?'

'But——' The younger girl hesitated, as if gathering her thoughts together. 'I can't blame him for wanting what's best for both of us—and it must be that, because he wouldn't want a brother-in-law he didn't like!'

As Verona sighed in exasperation at the Greek girl's resignation, Katina flashed her an understanding smile. 'Do you know Andreas was only twenty-two when my father was drowned? He'd only just finished his National Service so he'd no recent experience in the business, but that didn't stop him accepting responsibility for it, despite the fact that Uncle Yorgos advised him to sell out. He thought Andreas was too young and inexperienced to gain the respect and loyalty of a fair-sized workforce, but Andreas was determined to make a success of it for Mama's sake.'

'Good for him,' Verona dismissed Andreas's achievement drily. What a gift for a young man—to walk into an established company and sit back and collect the profits!

'It wasn't easy!' The note of reproof in the other girl's voice told Verona she hadn't been as clever in concealing her cynicism as she'd intended. 'Of course, I was only a child at the time, but Mama told me later how hard he worked to keep the company functioning, how he took courses in management and marketing, sitting up all hours of the night to study and how, when other young men were taking wives and families, Andreas spent long hours delving into the company's records, identifying high profitability areas and researching new openings for its range of textiles.'

A smile touched Verona's mouth at Katina's enthusiasm. 'He's a lucky guy to have such an admiring sister,' she opined.

'Not lucky—worthy,' the Greek girl corrected. 'He's put in a great deal of hard work, and it's only in these past few years he's really seen his dreams begin to materialise. Last year he signed a contract with Vayne Productions to supply all the fabrics for their next two productions...'

'Vayne Productions? The film people?' Surprise made Verona interrupt, impressed at last. 'Good heavens, that *was* an achievement!'

Katina smiled triumphantly at the note of genuine admiration in Verona's response. 'Chigwell Vayne's got a holiday home here in Crete—that's how he discovered Constanidou Textiles, but the contract wasn't a gift, I can promise you!' Excitement coloured her soft voice.

'Now, with Greece in the Common Market, Andreas is making plans for further expansion in Europe as well as talking about setting up a subsidiary in the States to keep his grip on the film industry.'

'That's marvellous, Kati.' Verona helped herself to another chunk of the delicious Greek bread. She'd had no idea of the size of the family textile company, believing it to be no more than a small local factory. However, his success didn't excuse Andreas Constanidou's behaviour towards herself, though it did go some way to explaining his high-handedness, she allowed. At the level he operated, he had to be used to making snap judgements.

Thoughtfully Verona pursed her lips. She only hoped, for the continuing prosperity of his business, that he wasn't always as mistaken as he'd been in her case. 'But it's no reason for marrying you off...'

'He feels responsible for me! Oh, can't you see, Verona?' Katina leaned over the table, her face flushed and earnest. 'Andreas has been like a father to me, but he has his own life to lead. Now Mama has gone I'm a physical burden to him as well as a financial one. He can't take me with him when he travels abroad, and he won't leave me alone and unprotected here. Besides,' she added painfully, 'the house in Rethymnon where Mama and I lived has been sold, and the only other places I could stay are here and Andreas's apartment in Iraklion, and neither are really convenient.'

'Yes, I see.' Verona smiled ironically. A young sister about the place would certainly cramp Andreas's style. Katina might be naïve enough to believe that her brother wanted her married only for business purposes, but she, Verona, suspected his motives were far more personal. After all, the seaside villa and the city apartment were ideal love-nests for a successful company director with more than his fair share of good looks! 'But, Kati, you can't just bow down to Andreas's wishes regardless of how you feel yourself.' Verona heaved an exasperated sigh. 'Don't you want to fall in love?'

The younger girl's solemn eyes met and held her own. 'Aunt Irini says love comes after marriage, when you begin to live together, and Andreas...'

'Yes?' Verona raised a querulous eyebrow as Katina paused. 'I can't wait to hear your brother's philosophy on matters of the heart.'

'Andreas says that love is not to be trusted,' Katina said quietly.

'Speaking from his own experience, no doubt,' returned Verona cynically, wondering just how extensive that experience had been over the years.

'I don't know.' The younger girl shook her head. 'But Aunt Irini and Uncle Yorgos's marriage was arranged by their families and they're very happy together...' A slight quiver in her voice belied her equanimity, and Verona was quick to respond to it, reaching across the table to cover Katina's hand with her own.

'Katina, look... I don't deny that Andreas has been a caring brother to you, but there are limits to what he can morally expect from you in return, and if you're not prepared to tell him that, then I will!'

'No, Verona, please! You mustn't!'

'You're afraid of him!' It was an indictment as Verona frowned into the pale, worried face of her friend.

'No, not really...' The Greek girl stumbled for words. 'It's just that, even though he's my brother, I don't know him all that well. He's a lot older than I am and we haven't really seen all that much of each other but—but he's my only real relation apart from Aunt Irini, and I don't want to lose him!' She swallowed as if fighting back tears. 'Promise me, Verona, you won't do anything to upset him...please?'

It was a little late to make such a request of her, but Katina wasn't to know that. Besides, upsetting Andreas was one thing, alienating him from his young sister was something quite different; but, to do him justice, she suspected the arrogant Greek's sense of family was far too strong to be assailed by an outsider.

'I promise to keep your best interests at heart,' she compromised smoothly, praying inwardly that Aunt Irini might have been mistaken or Andreas's plans not materialised as he'd hoped. Ten days without a word from him... The outlook for Katina might be brighter than she imagined!

Deciding to change the subject before Katina tried to elicit a more specific promise from her, Verona rose to her feet.

'I can't wait to get to that beach you were telling me about yesterday,' she announced brightly. 'A morning of sun and solitude is just what I need at the moment.'

To her surprise, Katina made a rueful grimace.

'Would you mind if I didn't come with you? I think I had a little too much sun yesterday. My head feels a bit muzzy. I thought I'd spend the day here, take a couple of aspirins and do some reading.'

'Of course!' Verona was immediately sympathetic. 'We can go any time. I'll stay here with you.' With a feeling of irritation Verona saw that there were shadows under the younger girl's eyes which hinted at the possibility that she was not as resigned to accepting an unknown bridegroom as she'd persuaded herself.

'Oh, no, there's no need for that!' Katina's smile removed any sting from her reply. 'I'd prefer to be alone.

I've got a couple of books I bought at Gatwick which I've never got round to reading.' She reached for the bag at her feet to produce two paperbacks. 'It'll give me a nice virtuous feeling to know I'm practising my English.'

Intrigued, Verona took the books from her unresisting hands.

'Oh, Kati!' she laughed, looking at the lurid covers with a mixture of amusement and horror—*Admissions of Aphrodite* and *A Question of Virtue*!

'Well, we did Shakespeare and Charles Dickens at college.' Katina defended her choice with a grin. 'I fancied something a little more contemporary.'

When their mutual laughter had subsided, Katina told Verona about the beach: where it was and how it could only be reached from the sea or by walking round the base of the sea-washed cliffs.

Two hours later she was stretched out on her towel on the deserted beach, offering the backs of her legs and the long, exposed curve of her back to the sun.

If Katina hadn't let her into the secret, she'd never have discovered the small, isolated bay at all. It had taken twenty minutes of treading on underwater rocks made slippery by seaweeds, jumping from one craggy foothold to another until eventually she'd stepped down on to the firm, cool base of white sand and realised with a thrill of achievement that she'd arrived.

How long she'd been bathing in those perfect surroundings she didn't know. It hadn't been just physically refreshing; it had been spiritually uplifting, too. Invaluable for healing the ego Andreas had bruised with his unwarranted accusations and atavistic brutality.

Turning over, Verona flung an arm across her eyes to reinforce the protection already afforded by her mirrored sunglasses. Hopefully, whatever was keeping

Andreas in Iraklion—or perhaps, she amended cynically, *whoever*—would continue to do so until her conscience allowed her to return to England.

Unbidden, the memory of his body pressing her into
the softness of the armchair leapt to her mind. For ten
days she'd steadfastly refused to remember the incident.
Now it forced itself on her. Oh, God! The wicked ex-
pertise of that kiss! The sheer, practised sensuality had
been an insult in itself when inflicted so scorn-
fully...and yet...

She'd been mad to taunt him. She ought to have realised he'd see any sign of criticism as an invitation for
abuse. Experience and common sense should have
warned her that Andreas Constanidou had little in
common with the conventional earnest, boring young
men she'd worked with at Consolidated Industries.

Oh, how could she have let him make such a fool of
her?

'No...no...' she moaned aloud, lost in her thoughts,
rejecting not only the unwelcome realisation that the
tyrannical Greek had aroused her hidden sensual nature,
but the memory of the entire shaming incident.

'I haven't even asked you yet.'

Verona cried out with shock as the deep voice, instantly recognisable, spoke from a few feet in front of
her. Her body jack-knifed up, arms caressing bent knees
in a protective manner. Her heart hammering with the
double shock of finding herself not alone and with him
of all people, plus the embarrassment of his having heard
her speaking to herself, she forgot the resolution she'd
made to remain icily detached in his presence in any
future confrontation.

'What are you doing here?' she demanded crossly.

'Being refused, by the sound of it,' he replied amiably, obviously not in any way disturbed by her unfriendly greeting.

Wearing black satin bathing shorts neatly elasticated round his trim waist, the bottoms 'V'-notched for freedom of movement, revealing the full muscled length of long, powerful legs, Andreas contemplated her with a disturbing half-smile.

Fighting to regain her composure, Verona continued to appraise him, confident that behind her mirrored lenses the direction of her eyes couldn't be detected.

He was, she admitted grudgingly, as good to look at undressed as he was dressed—if one liked the archetypal Greek God concept. He was also, not surprisingly, wet. Water dripped from his hair, which lay in disarming curls on his forehead, and ran down his neck. Her hidden gaze followed the small rivers as they coursed over his collarbones, streamed over the firmly developed chest, flowing each side of the small, hard male nipples to tease their way through the fine line of dark hair that started at chest-level, arrowing downwards to be engulfed by the satin trunks, only to appear again on each hard thigh as a light, silky adornment on the brown satin skin beneath them.

It was all she could do to stop herself from putting her hand against her own chest, where her heart was beating far too fast for comfort.

'I'm sorry if I startled you—I thought you knew I was here.' Andreas smiled with infuriating humour. 'You must have been dreaming behind those disconcerting lenses.' He nodded at the sunglasses.

'A nightmare would be a better description,' she murmured, inwardly amused at how near the truth he'd been, but determined not to be overtly friendly.

'Really?' He raised an expressive eyebrow. 'It's very unwise to sleep on the beach, you know. Apart from the possibility of a nasty sunburn, it can conjure up all sorts of hallucinations. What was yours, I wonder, Verona? Did you dream you were Andromeda chained to a rock, waiting for your fate?'

'Something like that,' she accorded pleasantly. If it pleased him to allude to Greek legends, she was quite happy to go along with him.

'And then you awakened to find me standing over you!' He laughed down at her, perfect teeth a flash of white against the smoothly tanned skin of his face. 'No wonder you screamed.' His gaze was openly mocking. 'Tell me, was it because you saw me as Perseus come to save you—or the sea-monster come to devour you?'

'Ah...' Gradually Verona was beginning to relax after the shock of his arrival, and the conversation had its amusing angle. She tilted her blonde head to one side. 'If you're asking me which would be worse—marrying you or being eaten by you—then I must admit I'd find both alternatives equally unattractive.'

'Would you?' He sounded genuinely amused. 'Then let me tell you, in either role, I fancy I'd be facing an indigestible task!'

Despite her resolve not to drop her guard against him, she felt her lips start to quiver.

'Are you laughing with relief, or crying with disappointment?' Before she could gather her startled wits together, Andreas dropped down on his haunches in front of her and whipped off the sunglasses.

'Andreas!' she protested angrily, reaching forward as he held them behind his back.

'I want to see your eyes.' There was no trace of apology as his own light gaze sought hers.

Defiantly she closed her eyes, protecting them against the sudden onrush of brilliance. It went against the grain to plead with him, but she had no option. 'Please, Andreas—I need them.'

'Endaxi!' He produced them from behind his back, placing them gently on the small bridge of her straight pretty nose. 'You shall have them now, but later, when we talk, you will take them off. There's no pleasure for me in talking to my own reflection.'

Verona remained obdurately silent. She'd no intention of following any such dictate unless it pleased her to do so. On the other hand, she didn't want to invite open warfare at this time and in this lonely place by expressing her cynical surprise at his dislike of looking at his own image! He still hadn't explained his presence there, anyway.

'So you left Katina alone at the villa?' The question was deceptively mild as in a simple, fluid movement he spun round to sit down beside her sharing her towel.

'Yes.' She edged away, all too aware of the lazy power that emanated from his relaxed form. He must have gone directly to the villa where Katina had told him of her destination. Had she also told him that it was on her insistence that Verona had left her alone? Or was she in for another insulting lecture about her responsibilities?

'She's suffering from a slight headache,' she said stiffly at last, hating the need to justify her actions but deciding that discretion was the better part of valour where her arrogant companion was concerned.

'Mmm,' he agreed drily. 'So she said.'

Flushing slightly, Verona glanced away, aware that her attempt to be placatory had amused him.

After a slight pause he said thoughtfully, 'Kati seems to have settled back here very well. I thought she seemed to be in excellent spirits.'

Verona nodded her agreement, eager to confirm his opinion. 'It's been a happy time for both of us, having fun in this beautiful place, doing what we liked, when we liked ... that is ...' For a moment, in her enthusiasm, she'd forgotten to be on the defensive. She stopped abruptly.

'That is—within the limits I suggested to you,' Andreas finished her sentence smoothly. 'Is that what you were going to say?'

'No!' Verona denied it vigorously. 'At least, only as far as they were in accordance with my own wishes!' Heatedly she faced him, this time removing her own sunglasses so her angry eyes could flare the truth of her statement directly into his cool, blue-eyed perception.

'Is that so?' It was said musingly, and it was all Verona could do not to lash out at the supercilious smile bestowed on her.

'Look ...' she retorted, incensed anew by the laughing disbelief she could read on his arrogant face, 'I've stayed here for Katina's sake, but it's becoming increasingly difficult ...'

'To give up the pleasures of the flesh?' he drawled cynically, watching with close interest the angry flush that spread across her face.

'To convince you I came here in good faith, that I never lied to your aunt—or to anybody else for that matter!' Unbearably provoked, her voice rose dramatically.

'I know you didn't lie to my aunt.'

Andreas made the statement so coolly, so calmly that she had to fight down a rising hysteria as she rose to her feet and glared down at his lazily sprawled body.

'You—what?' she choked.

'Know you didn't lie to Aunt Irini,' he repeated silkily, rising to his own feet to stand squarely facing her. 'That's one of the reasons I came here to see you.'

There was such a look of bland self-satisfaction on his dark face now, she could cheerfully have throttled him.

'Go on,' she gritted.

'I phoned her up again and asked her where she got your supposed description.'

'And?' she asked eagerly.

'She said when I asked her to describe "this tutor of Katina's", she was so distressed because of Yorgos's illness that she didn't make the obvious connection between my question and the friend Katina wanted to bring here. She thought I was asking for a description of Katina's lecturer in Advanced English for Foreigners.'

'Mrs Williams!' Torn between relief, amusement, horror and righteous indignation, Verona could only stand gaping into Andreas's face. 'She described Mrs Williams!' How stupid of her not to have realised when Andreas had first relayed the information to her.

'So it would seem.' His eyes laughed unrepentantly into hers, causing a strange quivering feeling to erupt in her stomach.

'Another small error of judgement?' Her mouth curled in derision at the prospect of humbling him.

A grin pulled the corner of his mouth upwards and she found the crooked smile devastatingly effective, but it would take a lot more than a formal apology before she'd be prepared to forgive him for the treatment he'd

meted out so unjustly. Come to that—she'd no clear rec-
ollection of having been given an apology...

'A misunderstanding,' he corrected gravely. Then, as
her mouth opened to protest, 'And one for which I take
full responsibility.'

Looking defiantly into his lean, attractive face, Verona
experienced the visual shock and quickened heartbeat
that had afflicted her at the first sight of him at the
airport. With the strong sunlight highlighting the bur-
nished smoothness of his skin, droplets of water
glistening in the exposed hollows of his face and body,
he was a formidable adversary—and a totally impeni-
tent one at that!

For the sake of her own dignity, he mustn't be allowed
to see the effect he was having on her: so her voice was
casually unemotional as she continued her cool regard.
'I'm delighted you acknowledge your mistake. Now you
know I'm a fit companion for your sister, you'll be saved
all the inconvenience of having to make regular checks
on my behaviour.'

A flicker of amusement touched his eyes before fading
as he told her softly, 'Ah, but the question of your suitability hasn't altered, I'm afraid.'

For a split second his response stunned her as she tried
to grapple with the injustice of his attitude. 'But—but
you just admitted...'

'That you didn't lie to get the job,' he finished for her
with easy nonchalance. His lazy shrug drew her bewildered glance to his naked, powerful shoulders. 'But the
fact remains, if I'd any idea at all what you looked like,
you'd never have been engaged.'

Verona shook her head in silent desperation, taking
the opportunity to replace her sunglasses. It was too
absurd for words to pre-judge her in this way. Just be-

cause she was a young and reasonably attractive woman, he'd formed the opinion she was only too eager to involve herself in God knew what kind of relationships with men. Presumably he was basing his prejudices on the observed behaviour of other female tourists, but it was hardly a scientific sample!

It was true, she admitted, there'd been plenty of opportunity for flirting if she'd been so inclined. Andreas had described accurately the type of advances the two girls might encounter and these had certainly materialised, but never to the degree where they'd become objectionable, or where a polite but firm refusal had been ignored.

She'd also seen the lengths to which some couples were prepared to take their physical involvement with each other in public, and could readily understand why Andreas would frown on his sister or her friend's becoming involved in similar relationships, particularly in view of his own plans for Katina's future! But nothing was further from her mind than getting personally involved with a man and neglecting her friend.

'So are you here to apologise—or to replace me?' The bite was back in her tone with a vengeance.

'Certainly not to replace you, *yatáki mou*,' he answered swiftly, as his gaze wandered impertinently over her, lingering thoughtfully on the black nylon satin of her one-piece swimsuit. 'Perhaps I came to see if you were obeying my instructions about not sunbathing topless.'

'And perhaps you were surprised?' she shot back furiously. 'Or even disappointed?'

A muscle jerked in his jaw, and not for the first time was she grateful for the anonymity the sunglasses afforded her.

'Surprised, yes,' he admitted, his mouth twitching with curbed laughter. 'I had a feeling you couldn't wait for an opportunity to defy me. But disappointed? Definitely not. When the time comes for me to enjoy the sight of your unclad body it will give me the greatest pleasure to know it's a privilege not already extended to the community in general and my fellow countrymen in particular.'

Verona's jaw dropped open as, hardly able to credit her ears, confusion overtook her. How dared he assume that at some later date she'd allow him to see her in anything less than she had on at that moment? To her consternation she felt a warm tide of colour being born somewhere in the region of her navel, stretching out its crimson fingers towards her face.

There was only one thing to do. She must ignore the implication of his pointed comment.

'You don't share your fellow countrymen's admiration of the "topless tourist"?' she queried with assumed sang-froid, and watched his lips clamp reflectively.

'If by that you mean, do I stare at the array of half-naked women stretched out on our beaches, then the answer is—of course I do.' The fact that he was openly laughing at her only increased Verona's feeling of frustration. 'But the point about that is, they aren't Greek women. Some of them may, during their brief stay, invade our thoughts, even our beds, but they won't share our lives and become the mothers of our children. They aren't *our* women.'

His eyes were blue lasers piercing through the protective glass that hid her reaction. 'I know of no Greek who would allow his woman to flaunt herself in such a manner.' His tone was calmly informative. 'In fact, the local papers will bear witness to the fact that some women have had their throats cut by their husbands for much less provocative behaviour.'

Verona heaved in a deep breath, aware that she was witnessing a manifestation of the attitude existing in what was still a male-dominated society.

'I don't doubt it,' she said drily. 'But then *I'm* not Greek, nor am I anybody's woman, as you so charmingly put it. Therefore, there should be no such arbitrary constraints on how I choose to sunbathe.'

The sentence finished in a gasp as Andreas's hand closed on her shoulder.

'You are a temporary member of my household. I decide what constraints apply to you.' She could feel the keen, penetrating eyes burning into her as she stiffened and tried to pull away from him. 'If you choose not to obey me, then you must be prepared to take the consequences.'

'And risk getting my throat cut?' she mocked him, but was unable to hide the pulse of apprehension that beat at the base of her throat.

For a moment there was only silence between them. Then Andreas asked softly, 'So that's the way it is, *yatáki mou*. You're looking for a confrontation, are you? You want to fight me, hmm?'

CHAPTER FOUR

DISCONCERTINGLY aware that the gleam in Andreas's compelling eyes was creating havoc with her autonomic nervous system, Verona dropped her gaze from his smouldering regard. Why did she have the strangest feeling he would welcome conflict with her, that battle and victory were an essential part of his complex nature—stimulants to his aggressive male ego?

Well, that was one satisfaction she could deny him—for the time being.

'Not on this point,' she retorted coolly. 'I never had any intention of sunbathing topless, regardless of your opinion. It's not a question of modesty—simply practicality! My skin's very fair and burns easily. It would be stupid to expose parts of my body which are covered all the year to the rays of the Mediterranean sun.'

'Very wise.' Andreas's dark head nodded as her mouth tightened. Impossible to miss the complacency behind the reply, which insinuated that he still thought he'd engineered her surrender with his implied threats.

She bit back any verbal retaliation. Silence would be more dignified.

'And, now we're agreed on that,' Andreas continued easily, choosing to ignore the muted antagonism on her set face, 'I can tell you the real reason I came here was to take you out to lunch.'

'Oh!' As her shoulder was released, Verona swung her other hand up to comfort the sensation his touch had left on her tender skin. He hadn't said so, but this invitation must be his way of apologising for calling her a liar.

At least, she admitted in his favour, he'd had the grace to tell her he'd discovered the truth. Heaven knew, she didn't want to spend any more time in his abrasive company than absolutely necessary, and he couldn't force her to eat with him.

On the other hand, perhaps she owed it to herself to show a little courtesy, if only to create a precedent between them!

'Thank you,' she made herself reply stiffly. 'That would be very pleasant.'

Although he'd swum round the cliffs, when Andreas heard she had walked he insisted on walking back the same way with her, for she expressed her doubts about coping with the large outcrops of undersea rocks if she followed his example.

His very presence was unnerving, as he stayed so close to her that she was constantly aware of his lean, hard body brushing her own. There was no way of knowing if it was deliberate contact, and she felt obliged to give him the benefit of the doubt. But she'd wanted to avoid all physical contact with him and he was making it exceedingly difficult!

Even as she dwelt on the matter he leaped nimbly in front of her, to land squarely on the surface of a triangular-shaped, uneven rock around the base of which the sea swirled and eddied with an alarming sucking noise, holding out his hand.

'Here——' he invited encouragingly. 'Take hold—I'll help you across.'

Verona looked doubtfully at the distance from where she stood and the rough surface she was being asked to attain.

'I'd rather walk nearer to the cliff,' she said hesitantly.

Andreas peered down into the water. 'With all that seaweed?' His dark head shook knowledgeably. 'You'll slip.'

'No, I won't, I—o-o-oh!' She'd taken her hand off the supporting cliff, and as she turned her head to speak her foot had indeed slipped, plunging her sideways.

Reflexes lightning-swift, Andreas jumped from his perch into waist-deep water, catching her firmly round the armpits, sweeping her away from the danger of bruising herself on the rocks as she fell.

It all happened so quickly that Verona found herself clinging to him before she realised exactly how she'd got into his arms.

Andreas had jumped into the gritty base between two outcrops of rock, and now, his feet firmly braced against the swell and suck of the sea as it harried the point between the two beaches, he held her pressed hard to his own body, her feet clear of the sea-bed, her own slender form being drawn by suction to mould closer and closer to that of her rescuer.

At the worst, she'd been in danger of grazing herself as she fell. The situation she now found herself in was decidedly more perilous!

'Thank you,' she muttered, hardly recognising her own voice. 'Could you put me down now, please?'

Andreas obeyed her, sliding her gently down his own body until her feet rested by his own, but his hands continued to hold her. Above the waterline her skin burned against his, on fire from the sun and the scorching touch of his naked flesh. Beneath the water their limbs intertwined, obeying the will of the current that forced them to acknowledge the difference in their shapes, pulling curve to hollow, fitting them together like the inter-locking pieces of a jigsaw.

'Verona...' Her name was a breath on his tongue, then he'd turned her in his arms, one hand going up to support her head, the other behind her back as he lowered his face and took her mouth with his own.

He was trembling and his kiss tasted of the sea, the sun and the indefinable excitement that was the essence of Andreas himself. Warm and seductive, his mouth plundered hers, persuading her to give freely of its hidden bounty, until Verona gasped for breath beneath the excess of his demands.

At last his lips released their claim, teasing her dazed, pulsating mouth with a gentleness that was almost an apology.

Bewildered and confused by the suddenness of what had erupted between them, Verona felt a shiver of apprehension tremble down her spine. There was nothing she could say, and the only thing she could do was to move away from him, away from the powerful length of his lean male body which had spoken to her as clearly as his mouth and with a message equally unacceptable.

Dear heavens! This was Andreas Constanidou, brother to the girl for whom she was to provide a chaste and proper escort. Of all people, he was the last, the absolute last, she could allow to arouse such strange longings and emotions that now coursed through her.

Valiantly she strove to remind herself that *this* was the domestic tyrant whose rumoured intentions for his young sister she abhorred. It was nothing short of treason for her heart to pound with this primeval awareness of his attractiveness, or for her blood to sing in her veins as if she'd just discovered some fount of endless joy!

Her confusion was mirrored in the depths of her eyes as she gazed at Andreas in shocked dismay. She'd begun to hope that his opinion of her had risen since their first turbulent interview, but what had just happened between them proved that to be a forlorn supposition. Apparently he still saw her as an available commodity.

When he extended a damp forefinger with a thoughtful slowness to stroke one of her flushed cheeks, she could only stare appealingly at him, praying she was not to be insulted because of her inexplicable response to his unexpected caresses.

The dark fan of his lashes masked the expression of his eloquent eyes as Andreas murmured softly, 'You see what I mean?' The broken huskiness of his voice was accusation enough. 'You're not suitable for this job, *yatáki mou*. Not suitable at all!'

The terrace of the restaurant was perched on a plateau of rock overlooking the valley between two mountain ridges. Thick vines grew up the side walls to cover the bamboo trellis overhead, and already Verona could see the young bunches of grapes forming.

She stared up at them, glad to look anywhere rather than meet Andreas's gaze across the small table.

If there'd been any way she could have refused his invitation after the incident in the sea, without betraying her feelings to Katina, she would have done so.

Once they'd regained the main beach, she'd located her *pareo* and sandals from their hiding place, reknotting the fabric at shoulder and hip to form an instant open-sided dress, well aware that Andreas, who'd watched the transformation with intense interest, could hardly have missed the way her fingers trembled at their task.

Afterwards he'd walked back with her in the simmering heat to the villa and waited patiently while she'd
showered and changed, chatting to Katina, who had refused an invitation to accompany them.

What she'd really needed was to be by herself for long
enough to evaluate the importance of how she'd felt,
locked in Andreas's arms, conscious of his need to
possess her and her own momentary mindless response
to his overpowering charisma, but it had been denied
her.

Sitting silently beside him in the car, she'd wished with
all her heart she didn't have to face the ordeal of a meal
with him, having to pretend that nothing untoward had
happened between them, when every fibre of her being
condemned her assumed calmness. How could she
possibly relax enough to eat when her mind was in such
a turmoil?

So when he asked if she had a preference she'd shaken
her head, suggesting hopefully, 'Something light—I'm
not very hungry.'

'*Endaxi*.'

To her relief he accepted her request. She'd half
expected him to try and force food into her the same
way he seemed determined to force his opinions down
her throat!

Waiting for the meal to be served, she smiled to herself.
In this instance she'd done him an injustice, but it didn't
alter the fact that he still regarded her as an unwelcome
visitor to the villa. The memory of his stern dismissal
of her suitability for the post of Katina's companion still
rankled bitterly, making it impossible for her to relax
and enjoy the beautiful surroundings. Damn it! Anyone
would think she'd slipped off that wretched rock on
purpose!

At that moment her troubled thoughts were distracted by the arrival of the meal Andreas had chosen for both of them—two long wooden skewers threaded with chunks of crisply grilled meat, together with a communal bowl of salad, a basket of bread and a round deep dish containing a delicious-smelling sauce.

'You have to use your fingers.' Andreas broke the silence, demonstrating his words by easing off the nearest piece of meat on his own skewer, dipping it into the sauce and neatly biting it in half. Cool eyes glinted at her beneath his soft lashes as she watched every movement of his long, capable fingers and the sharp efficiency of those perfect teeth. 'Poor Verona—you find our customs very old-fashioned, not to say uncivilised, don't you?'

'No.' She denied it quickly, copying his action, while he watched her with the hint of a smile curling his sensuous mouth.

'You know there's an old Cretan saying—"A man's hand discovers heaven when it touches tender meat or the flesh of a beautiful woman."' He sighed. 'Today fortune indeed smiles on me—I have found heaven more than once.'

Discomfited by the sudden teasing note in his deep voice, Verona shot Andreas a look meant to quell, but he refused to be abashed.

'Can't you forgive me for one mistake?'

One mistake! As far as his opinion of her was concerned, it was riddled with mistakes! Resolutely she pushed aside the nagging thought that her own behaviour at the airport might have been misleading. If he hadn't been on the prowl she wouldn't have looked at him twice!

'I wasn't aware you were seeking absolution,' she retorted tartly as with grim determination she lifted a wedge of tomato from the salad dish.

'Of course you were,' he said calmly. 'But you're still very angry with me because I put Katina's interests before yours.' He concentrated on removing another succulent piece of meat from his skewer, transferring it to his mouth.

Tight-lipped, Verona sat watching the manoeuvre. Katina's interests were the same as hers as far as she was concerned! But who was going to believe that? Certainly not the overbearing Greek sharing her table!

When he could speak again, Andreas continued smoothly, 'On many occasions authority is an irksome burden but, where my sister is concerned, protecting her is a pleasure as well as a duty, and you must allow me to be the best judge of how this is done.'

He searched her face for signs of argument but, finding none, appeared to relax.

'You see, Katina has led a very restricted life—much more so than is normal, even in Greece. She was only six when our father was killed in a diving accident. It was two days before his body was found, and the strain of praying and waiting for news nearly destroyed Mama's sanity. Afterwards she seemed to lose all interest in life, devoting herself to Katina and guarding and protecting her as if she might be snatched away at any second.'

Memories etched lines of grief on his face as he continued speaking, leaning across the table to ensure Verona's avid attention.

'I didn't like what I saw, but there was little I could do apart from ensuring Kati received a good education. So much of the time I had to be away on business, and I comforted myself by believing she never showed any signs of unhappiness at being deprived of the company of her contemporaries out of school hours—that she was happy in her isolated environment.'

'Go on,' Verona encouraged him softly as he paused. 'Katina's never spoken to me about her early life.' And she'd never asked, some premonition warning her that the Greek girl preferred not to discuss it.

'There's not a lot more to tell.' Andreas shrugged his broad shoulders. 'As the years went by, Mama came to depend more and more on Kati's company. When I was home I tried to see she had some social life, but when I was away Kati seemed content to spend all her time with Mama.

'As I told you, when she had her fatal stroke Kati was alone in the house with her. She did everything possible, but there'd never been the slightest chance of survival. Afterwards Kati seemed to lose all her strength and vitality. It was as if she'd lost all reason for living.' For a moment he remained silent, contemplating the past before resuming. 'It was then that the doctor suggested she make a complete break with the past. Yorgos and Irini were only too glad to give her a temporary home in England, and Kati . . . well, Kati didn't care what happened to her at the time. The rest you know.'

'She made a marvellous recovery.' Verona had been contrasting the introverted, shy teenager of a year ago with the lovely girl Katina had become over the months of their friendship. There was certainly nothing morbid about her now, but for the first time Verona began to appreciate Andreas's concern about his sister's homecoming: the deeper reasons behind his wanting her to have a reliable companion while he, himself, had to be away working.

He nodded his agreement. 'Thank God, yes. Being with a family, becoming concerned with their business, making friends, all worked wonders. But after the first few months all she really wanted to do was return to Crete. I could feel her homesickness, her pain in the letters she wrote, but I was afraid she might succumb to the old depression.'

'So you persuaded Yorgos and Irini to come back with her.' Verona nodded understandingly, adding the silent rider—after you'd put events in motion to provide her with a permanent companion to take her off your hands completely.

'It seemed the ideal solution.' Andreas made a grimace. 'Irini was just the stable, middle-aged influence I believed Katina needed. Someone who would care for her and advise her. Their son Petros could manage the restaurant in their absence and and the villa would sleep three.' He sighed, his mouth turning with a half-humorous twist. 'Who could have guessed poor Uncle Yorgos would catch *arnemovlogia*!'

It sounded even worse in Greek than English! A qualm of conscience struck Verona for Katina's hapless relative, her mind momentarily diverted from the planned treachery that Andreas had still not mentioned.

'How is he, have you heard?' she asked with genuine concern, knowing that the childhood disease could be quite nasty for adults.

'Much better, but unfortunately he's still not a pretty sight to look upon, according to my Aunt Irini.'

'I'm glad.' Verona responded, unable to control the wry grimace that turned down the corners of her mouth before adding hastily, 'About his recovery, not his appearance.'

'If that's glad, *yatáki mou*, how does sorry sound?'

Unable to meet Andreas's laughing regard across the table, Verona glanced down at her lap. 'I was just thinking that if it hadn't been for Uncle Yorgos's illness I might be starting on my new career at this moment.'

'Instead of relaxing in the sun?' His smile told her he couldn't believe she regretted the way fate had treated her. 'Kati told me you'd given up your job before she asked you to come here with her—why?'

'I was bored.' She decided not to prevaricate. 'I thought that by joining a large company I'd be able to put my qualifications to their best use, but it didn't work out that way. All the records were computerised and there was no personal contact with the staff at all—a zombie could have done my job!' Her voice grew impassioned. 'The pay and conditions were excellent, but it wasn't enough. I needed a challenge, to be stretched.' She raised her eyes to meet his frankly interested appraisal. 'Do you understand that?'

'Very much so.' Did she see a glimmer of a new respect for her on his personable face? 'And exactly what are these elastic qualifications which were under-used, hmm?'

Verona swallowed her disappointment as the cynicism of his reply dispelled her short-lived hopes of winning his respect. 'My degree was in sociology and business studies,' she informed him frostily. 'I chose the subjects to fit me for a career in commerce.'

'Ah . . . yes.' Andreas contemplated his empty plate, a small smile still playing about his lips. 'And it was in sociology you were lecturing when you first met Katina, was it not? You must be quite an expert.'

'Yes . . . and yes.' She met his enquiring look with a stony countenance. 'But the lecturing was merely a temporary job to help out a friend who was ill.'

'Lucky students, to have such an attractive teacher.' The blue eyes caressed her face thoughtfully. 'But a dangerous subject, I think, for the young and head-strong. Do you practise what you preached, *yatáki*?'

'It's a science, not a creed!' Verona flashed back, ir-ritated by his pet name for her, and prepared to justify the hours of studying and teaching she'd done over the past years. But Andreas wasn't going to give her the satisfaction of an argument, she realised as he shrugged his shoulders dismissively.

Verona's fingers gripped the edge of the table as she leaned towards him, determined to make her point of view known. 'It's a science based on group observation...'

'Ah!' His sharp exclamation stopped her midstream. 'Then I have a real treat in store for you—pleasure and research mixed.' A wicked triumph echoed in his deep voice. 'A business colleague of mine is giving a party tomorrow night, and I've accepted his invitation on behalf of Katina and yourself as well. Have you heard of Chigwell Vayne?'

'Yes—no—that is...' Confused, Verona halted to gather her wits together. Of course she'd felt a twinge of excitement at the news. Who wouldn't? After all, Chigwell Vayne was famous, not to say infamous! And it would certainly give her something to write about to her mother! Still, she'd have preferred to have been asked rather than informed.

Andreas had told her he was seeking absolution, but she'd seen no change in his attitude towards her to suggest he regarded her in a kindlier light. A man didn't have to like a woman in order to kiss her the way Andreas had seen fit to do a few hours earlier, nor did he have to respect her, Verona told herself grimly.

Deep inside her a flame of mutiny flared. There'd be a perverse pleasure in thwarting his plans. Certainly until she received a more genuine proof of his so-called contrition.

'Well—is it yes or no?' A querulous eyebrow demanded that she make herself clear.

'Yes, I've heard of him. And no, I don't wish to go to his party,' she returned succinctly.

'Then I must ask you to reconsider,' came a smooth reply. 'If not to please me...then for Katina's sake.'

'Kati hardly needs me if you're going to be there! And besides, I'm afraid my wardrobe doesn't include anything nearly glamorous enough for a Hollywood-style party.'

'But *I* need you to be there.' His uncompromising answer came back so quickly that Verona flinched. 'And as for your dress, since I shall be escorting you I shall make certain you're a credit to me.' The flashed smile on his arrogant face did nothing for Verona's pride as he continued smoothly, 'I'll choose what you wear and I'll pay for it.' One tanned hand waved away a minor hindrance to his plans with less effort than he would have accorded a mosquito. 'No problem.'

No problem, indeed! Verona gritted her teeth at the suave catchphrase. There were limits to what she'd suffer at the hands of Andreas Constanidou, and allowing him to choose her clothes was not included in the limited list.

'I'm sorry,' she told him icily. 'I prefer to stay in the villa by myself.'

A glimmer of humour lit the light eyes that raked her outraged face. 'And I want you to meet some very good friends of mine who have also been invited, so on this occasion I must insist your preferences take second place to my desire.'

He was being insufferable as usual, but what could she do? She wouldn't put it past him to leave Katina at home if she refused his demands, and that was a disappointment she couldn't visit on her friend.

She bit her lip angrily. If nothing else, this holiday was highlighting her own inadequacies, she acknowledged dourly, unable to remember a time when she'd felt so helpless.

'Has there ever been a time when they didn't?' she asked the implacable face regarding her across the table.

Andreas's slow, suggestive smile, the knowing glint in his remarkable eyes, caused a shiver to tremble down her rigidly held spine: both were as disturbing as his words.

'That's something you must answer for yourself, Verona,' he told her softly.

CHAPTER FIVE

'YOU look absolutely beautiful!' Katina, stunningly dressed in crimson silk, her dark hair swept to the top of her small head, surveyed Verona with patent admiration. 'And your dress is gorgeous!'

'Do you really like it?' Verona's perfect teeth bit her bottom lip gently as her brow furrowed in doubt. The soft apricot crêpe wasn't a colour she'd ever have chosen for herself, but it did echo and augment the warmth of her newly sun-kissed skin and tone in with the shining blonde tumble of curls that framed her oval face.

Sighing, she had to admit that some of her reservations sprang from the fact that she hadn't been consulted in its purchase!

It had been with barely concealed irritation that she'd allowed Andreas to take her into Iraklion after lunch the previous day. From the moment they'd stepped over the threshold of the exclusive shop, the proceedings had been taken completely out of her hands, Andreas and an elegant woman called Sophia, whom Verona supposed to be the manageress if not the owner, consulting with each other at great length to her exclusion.

Taken to a fitting-room where a number of dresses had been brought, she'd been helped to dress then reluctantly led out to parade up and down in front of Andreas, for whom an armchair had been conjured up in the main salon.

Her only consolation had been the absence of other customers to witness the exhibition she had provided.

76

When she had commented on this fact later to Andreas, he had shown mild surprise.

'But surely you realised Sophia saw us by special appointment? Only the tourist shops are open in Crete in the early afternoon.'

'Of course.' Kati's reply brought her back from yesterday's memories. 'It's perfect for you. Did Andreas select it?'

'It doesn't surprise you that he should?' Verona raised her eyebrows.

'Of course not!' Katina laughed away her friend's astonishment. 'He's got excellent taste. That's one of the reasons he's made such a big success of the business. It's not just his qualities for managership, but his ability to recognise and retain the best designers.' Her eyes darkened with mischief. 'I expect Sophia thought you were one of his ladyfriends.'

'Very probably, as he paid the bill!' Verona scowled at her reflection. It had been the impression she'd received as she'd been obliged to march up and down like some concubine showing off her charms for his approval. To have objected could only have worsened the situation, particularly as she'd had a strong feeling anything she'd said would have been ignored—even if it had been understood by the olive-skinned *vendeuse*. Now here was Kati insinuating that it was an often repeated occurrence!

Well, she determined, after the wretched party Andreas could have his dress back. If he was such a good customer, he might even be able to get his money refunded.

Brown and hazel eyes met in the mirror. 'He has lots of ladyfriends, does he?' Verona asked casually.

Katina's smile broadened, her small nose wrinkling with amusement. 'Do you doubt it? My Andreas is a

man, isn't he? Eventually he'll want to marry and have
sons, but now...' She shrugged expressive shoulders.
'He's free to look around, isn't he?'

And not only look, thought Verona pensively, turning
to assess her full reflection as she recalled with awesome
clarity the touch of his hands on her shoulders—the sensation of his hard, silky male mouth against her own
protesting lips... and the way the latter had ceased their
objection for an exhilarating moment of time....

Still, she had to admit she was pleased with her own
appearance. The crêpe formed a soft drape across the
commencing swell of her breasts before clinging to their
rounded outline, following the slender but rounded
curves of waist and hips before skimming the long reach
of her legs to swirl about her ankles. Even the way the
material plunged to her waist at the back was flattering
to the long, elegant sweep of her spine, the line of the
design being kept by slim strings of beaded crystal in
horizontal ladderback arrangement.

Despite her hesitancy about the colour, Verona had
to confess the whole effect was quite beautiful and she
felt good wearing it, although it would take her a little
time to get used to the friction of the material against
her naked breasts, since there was no bra designed that
could remain discreet beneath the cut-away back of the
style.

'You look absolutely stunning!' There was no doubting
the sincerity of Katina's compliment. 'I wouldn't be surprised if Andreas takes one look at you in that and falls
instantly in love!'

'If he does, then it's fated to remain unrequited!'

Verona's instant response was accompanied by a frown
assumed to punish Katina's impish grin. When she fell
in love, it wouldn't be with anyone as overpowering and

opinionated as the handsome Greek she'd agreed to work
for. No, she assured herself silently, her ideal mate would
be a man who would acknowledge and respect a woman
for her own qualities and treat her as his equal—not as
an accessory to his own image!

Two hours later she was taking another sip of champagne, exchanging a meaningless smile with the woman
seated to her right at the small table where she and Katina
had been taken by their host. Since then she'd not set
eyes on Andreas, who'd disappeared with Chigwell
Vayne into the darkened interior of the large house, built
like a medieval castle set against the backdrop of the
mountains with its paved floors, heavy wood and iron
chandeliers and arched windows.

Verona licked her lips indolently and gave a little sigh.
Before her, an olympic-size swimming pool glistened beneath a necklet of fairy lights. Beyond the surrounding
paved courtyards with their candlelit tables, landscaped
gardens terraced the mountain as far as the eye could
see beneath the starlit sky. The champagne both
quenched her thirst and aroused a desire for more—like
the kisses of a lover, she mused, smiling at her own
whimsy.

If she analysed her feelings—and there was little else
to do, since the conversation around her was taking place
in Greek—she had to admit to a sense of disappointment. Obviously she must have read too much in
Andreas's declaration of escorting her to the party. Now
she saw he'd meant he would take her there in her role
of chaperon and abandon her while he went about
finding his own enjoyment elsewhere! She'd been stupid
to hope for anything else.

At least Katina was enjoying herself. Verona looked at the bright eyes and animated countenance of her friend as she gazed into the face of the young Greek beside her. Stephanos Liviticos was an attractive young man with his curly black hair and liquid brown eyes, bearing a strong resemblance to his father seated on the other side of her.

These were the friends Andreas had wished her to meet. Perhaps he'd imagined they had some English or that Katina would act as interpreter or... and this was much more likely, she fumed... he didn't give a damn that she was bored and restless, excluded from the conversation through her own ignorance. Like an angel from heaven with her wings clipped, she thought sourly, listening to the music—turning her head to watch the couples dancing beneath the cantilevered canopy that extended from the house, while her pulses beat to the captivating rhythm of the band and her feet tingled to dance.

There remained the traditional escape route.

'Excuse me,' she murmured to the table at large. 'I'm just going to freshen up a little.'

'Well, well... has your escort deserted you so soon? It seems you keep him on too long a lead.'

Verona had been making the most of her freedom, standing back against one of the walls watching the circulating guests, her body swaying slightly to the beat of the music. At the sound of the laughing question addressed to her in a man's deep voice, she spun round in astonishment.

A slim, elegant young man a few inches taller than herself, with a lean, humorous face and a shock of streaked blond hair, met her surprised expression with a smile before bowing low in mock obeisance.

At least he spoke English, she registered thankfully, detecting a slight transatlantic accent.

'I'm afraid so,' she replied to his first question cheerfully. 'But I don't keep him on a lead, I'm afraid!' Her lips curved in amusement. Imagine any woman trying to take Andreas anywhere he didn't want to go!

'How unwise.' Brown eyes drifted over her with careful assessment. 'It seems he's allowed himself to be tempted to other pastures. How fortunate I happened to be passing. You can cry on my shoulder while we're dancing.'

He opened his arms to her invitingly, his mouth set in a boyish grin that was quite disarming.

'All right!' Verona warmed to his personality, as suddenly the evening seemed much brighter. 'Thank you. I'd love to dance.'

Holding her closely, her new partner moved her smoothly into the mass of dancers. 'So Constanidou's deserted you already. I must admit that's a record, even for someone with a reputation as a fast mover.'

Startled, Verona missed a beat, stumbled and apologised. 'He's a friend of yours?'

'I know him.' The reply was terse and non-committal. 'As a matter of fact, I saw you arrive with him and his little sister, and I have to admit to being intrigued.' He turned neatly at the edge of the floor, taking her easily towards the centre of activity with practised steps. 'Of course, it's common knowledge his recent girlfriend's been removed from his Iraklion apartment, but the consensus of opinion is that he's set her up in her own place somewhere discreetly in the background, so her presence won't disturb the little Katina now she's been permitted to return from exile.' He held her away from him, pursing his lips thoughtfully. 'But there's nothing on the

grapevine to suggest she's actually been displaced from
his—er—affections, shall we say, by another contender.
Then, lo and behold—you materialise on the scene. It's
enough to start all the tongues in Iraklion wagging.'

Torn between annoyance and amusement, Verona
raised her eyebrows in mock astonishment. 'It seems your
grapevine is rather out of date, since it doesn't carry the
news that Andreas Constanidou had engaged a chaperon
for his sister!'

'You're not...' Verona found herself brought to a halt
as her partner stared down at her. Then, as she nodded,
he gathered her into his arms again, holding her so close
she could feel his lean body shaking with laughter. 'My
God, but he's a crafty devil! Trust Constanidou to find
a way of having his cake and eating it too!'

Verona stiffened in his grasp. 'If you mean what I
think you do, then you owe me an apology,' she said
coldly. 'I can assure you there's no relationship between
Mr Constanidou and myself other than that of employer
and employee.' Not even friendship or mutual respect,
she qualified silently to herself, a spasm of misery
twisting unexpectedly in her heart. But it was imperative
for all their sakes that she stifled any source of false
rumours. 'To be honest with you, Mr Constanidou had
never set eyes on me before I arrived in Crete and, when
he did, he didn't want me,' she told him, her tone sharply
rebuking.

She heard his guffaw of laughter against her hair as
he spun her round in time to the music. 'There's really
no polite reply to that statement!' He was quite unrepentant. 'I can see you're not one of the usual crowd.
Where on earth did he find you?'

'I was teaching at the college Katina attended in
England,' Verona admitted, resigned now to answering

his questions and determined to carry out her own interrogation. 'What about you? Are you one of the *usual* crowd?'

'One of Chigwell's hangers-on, you mean?' He didn't wait for her confirmation. 'Yeah—that's me. Bob Grafton's the name. I rewrite deathless prose to make it instantly forgettable so it becomes suitable for epic production.'

'That sounds interesting.' Glad to move the conversation away from Andreas's private life, Verona encouraged his confidences. Why should she be interested in the woman he'd secreted away, anyway? At least it seemed he'd had the decency not to embarrass Katina by flaunting his affair in her face. There was no reason at all why she should have felt disturbed by the news.

'Yeah—isn't it?' Bob grinned down at her, happy to talk about himself. 'At the present time I'm rewriting the labours of Hercules. I'm slightly hampered for the time being because it hasn't been decided whether we go all-out for the macho image of the ancient Greeks, or make the whole thing allegorical by turning Hercules into a black athlete who has problems making the Olympics,' he explained drily.

'Oh, Bob...' Verona gurgled in delight at his droll expression, as he executed a neat turn and she began to enjoy herself for the first time that evening. 'Hasn't it all been done before?'

'Hasn't everything?' he countered cynically. 'There aren't any more virgin ideas around, any more than there are virgins themselves.'

'Perhaps that's simply because you don't know where to look for them.'

'Is that an invitation?'

'No!' She reproved him with mock sternness for his audacity. 'I merely meant that Greek families seem to take great care to protect their daughters' innocence.'

'Precisely,' he agreed triumphantly. 'Which is why they aren't "around" for public appraisal. They're married off in their cradles, then taught that their place in life is to be a good homemaker and mother, before being dispatched to the altar.'

'Surely arranged marriages aren't that prevalent in Greece?' Verona turned thoughtful eyes to scan his face.

Bob shrugged his shoulders. 'You'd be surprised! The women aren't forced into it, if that's what you mean. But I can assure you there's still a strong undercurrent of feeling, particularly in the Islands, that a girl should be guided by her family in anything so important. And let's face it—from the man's point of view it's ideal. What guy wouldn't like the opportunity of playing the field of foreign lovelies who flood these shores every summer, knowing full well, when he's bored with taking what's so freely offered, he can escape into the arms of a compliant, admiring virgin who will look on him as her master and her saviour?'

'Wow!' Verona's eyebrows shot up. 'And to think I considered Andreas Constanidou to be the prize chauvinist around!'

'All men are chauvinists at heart.' Bob bestowed a wry smile on her upturned face. 'It's only when they come to a country like Greece that they find the courage to admit it.'

For a few minutes they danced in silence before Bob said softly, 'Take your friend Constanidou, for example. Once he's got his little sister married off, in the traditional manner, he'll be free to marry his mistress at last, to give her the honour of bearing his name and the burden of his sons!' He laughed harshly. 'That's not to say he'll be faithful to her; but, being Greek, she'll turn a blind eye to his infidelities, safe in the knowledge that provided she behaves herself no one will ever take her place in his home.'

There was harsh, uncomfortable dryness in Verona's throat. Andreas wanted to marry the woman he was living with...to become a father? Was this the *true* reason behind his decision to introduce Katina to a husband? Yes, she acknowledged grimly, Andreas Constanidou would want to be the father of sons. He'd want to perpetuate the perfection of his lean, hard frame and handsome features, to obtain his own immortality through reproduction... Yes, she could find it easy to believe that Katina was to be sacrificed on the altar of Andreas's egotism...

'You seem to know him very well,' she offered at last, trying to hide her dismay.

'Well enough,' Bob conceded. 'Since Constanidou Textiles are contracted to Vayne Productions, our paths tend to cross from time to time—both commercially and socially.' His mouth twisted bitterly. 'I certainly wouldn't claim him as a friend—although we do have several friends in common, notably the lady who currently shares his bed—Yana Theodaxis.'

'Oh!' Verona stared at him with parted lips, uncertain how to respond. Uppermost in her mind was the knowledge that Bob Grafton had sought her out specifically to thrust the Greek girl's name at her. There was no denying the unhappiness lurking behind his dark gaze. She didn't need a degree in sociology to realise that whoever Yana was, she was more than just a 'friend' to Bob Grafton, or at least she had been, before moving in with Andreas.

Even as she watched Bob's face she saw the emotion there changing from misery to an almost malevolent amusement. 'Don't be too concerned for me, sweetheart. I shan't die of a broken heart. There are plenty more where she came from, and at least I deprived Constanidou of the satisfaction of being her first lover...although it seems he intends to be her last!'

'Are you sure?' Verona's sympathy for Bob's obvious jealousy was mixed with a mounting anger against Katina's brother, as she recalled his dictates as to her own behaviour.

He shrugged disconsolate shoulders. 'It's the first time he's ever shared his home with one of his lovers. Yana was staying at his Iraklion apartment before Katina was summoned home. Besides, she's Greek, and that's something new by all accounts. Most Greeks of his age have already sired their descendants, and it looks as if Constanidou isn't prepared to wait any longer to do the same. Our Andreas plays around with the tourists like most of his kindred, but, like them too, he believes in a pure blood-line. He'll want a Greek girl for the mother of his children—and he seems to have found the right one at last—damn him—although for a moment there I was hoping that you might have proved a diversion...'

'Oh, Bob, I'm sorry...' Verona sighed, putting out a sympathetic hand on his arm as the music stopped and they came to a halt by a slender pillar. Much as she resented being considered a possible 'diversion', she couldn't help feeling sorry for him, sorry for Katina and, for a reason she couldn't fathom—sorry for herself!

'Why couldn't I find a nice girl like you, little chaperon?' It was a soft murmur as the American saw the compassion and doubt on her expressive face.

Realising she'd never told him her name, Verona opened her lips to rectify the omission, only to have it stopped as he brought his mouth down to hers with a lingering kiss.

His lips were warm and dry. With the pillar pressed hard against her back there was nothing she could do to escape his unwanted attentions, so she bore the caress stoically, refusing to open her mouth to admit his questing tongue, glad he didn't try to force her. Nevertheless, lack of oxygen left her breathless when she was finally released.

Hands palmed against Bob's dinner-jacket, she raised accusing eyes to his face only to see he was looking over her shoulder, a smooth smile curving his wide mouth.

'Ah . . . Constanidou!' A gleam of smug satisfaction shone out behind the feigned courtesy of the greeting. 'I understand I have you to thank for bringing this lovely creature into my orbit!'

'No.' The Greek's languid tone was belied by the bright sparkle of animosity in his light eyes as Verona turned, gasping with shock at his unexpected arrival on the scene. 'Verona tends to be rather like a satellite without radio contact, veering off her planned course if she's not closely watched. In this instance, I can assure you, her orbit was very wide of the mark. Still,' he paused, drifting his gaze from Bob's flushed face to her own tense features, 'it's a situation that can easily be remedied by a little manual control.'

Every nerve of her body on edge, Verona stared at him in disbelief. 'Don't you dare lay a finger on me!' To her horror she heard her own voice quiver.

Expression inscrutable, he surveyed the apprehension in her lucid eyes. 'I was only suggesting we dance. Does the prospect strike so much fear into you?'

Damn his arrogance! She'd been intended to read a threat behind the words he'd thrown at the American, and this innocent reaction was merely for Bob Grafton's benefit. Neither was she unaware of the antagonism between the two men who stood on either side of her. It slumbered like a dormant volcano, and she didn't want to be around when it erupted!

'I'd prefer to go back to our table now.' She composed her voice, loosing herself from Bob's relaxed grip and turning to flay him with the hauteur of her expression. 'I enjoyed our conversation, Mr Grafton, but I don't like being used to pay off old scores.'

Abruptly she started out across the field of dancers, walking swiftly, head held high, ignoring Andreas's presence completely.

She'd barely gone more than a few yards before hard fingers spun her round and she was forced against the powerful frame of her employer as Andreas's arms encircled her.

His hand curved to her waist in a gesture of unchallenged possession, he forestalled the outburst trembling on her tongue. 'It seems I can't let you out of my sight for a few minutes without your running true to type.' The softness of his voice did nothing to hide its biting scorn as he drew his head back to study the defiance in her green-flecked eyes.

Stubbornly Verona refused him an immediate answer. Too conscious of his nearness and the effect it was having on her, she fought to control her body's wayward reactions, to settle the rapid beating of her heart and bring some strength back into her stumbling legs. How dared he demand that she explain her actions to him? What about his own plans for the desirable Yana and the result they would have on his young sister, only so recently recovered from a depression that could have ruined her future?

'It was more than a few minutes,' she accused eventually when she'd regained control over her voice. 'If you intended me to sit in one place all evening you should have made it clear at the start. It's a party, isn't it? I thought people were supposed to circulate!' Anger was a hard little knot somewhere beneath her breastbone as she raised her chin proudly, refusing to be cowed.

'You assumed my absence left you free to desert my sister and flirt with the first man who picked you up?' Light eyes sparkled with the fire of battle as Andreas voiced the question with sardonic intonation.

'That's monstrously unfair!' Verona snapped back angrily. 'In no way was Katina deserted. She couldn't have been better guarded if she were the Crown Jewels— surrounded as she was by your Greek friends.'

'You don't like the Liviticoses?'

She wasn't deceived by the bland tone of his question, as the pressure of his hand guiding her to the music tightened, emphasising his displeasure.

'I couldn't understand enough of what they said to form an opinion!' she declared mutinously. All her protective instincts warned her that to argue too fiercely with this man was dangerous and that he wouldn't hesitate to extract some penalty from her if she roused him too far; but she was beyond exercising caution, driven by a depth of anger she barely understood herself.

'At least you understood enough of what Bob Grafton said to know what he wanted—and to give it to him.'

She saw the light of contempt in his penetrating appraisal and responded wrathfully, her hazel eyes shooting flames of fury into his glowering face.

'I certainly understood enough of what he said to realise your "holier than thou" attitude is a big charade for Kati's benefit. I really don't see you have the right to question anyone else's behaviour when you're not above stealing another man's woman and setting her up in style somewhere behind his back!' she panted.

'So he talked to you about Yana Theodaxis, did he?' She wasn't misled by the thoughtful smile that twisted his mouth. The glint in those ice-blue eyes was sufficient evidence of his barely held temper. 'I don't suppose he told you that Yana is beautiful, intelligent and very talented, and he's not fit to share the same house as her...let alone the same bed!'

'Then it's fortunate you've provided her with another one, isn't it? I do admire the way you've kept it a secret from Katina...'

'Enough!'

The monosyllable silenced her with its sharpness as Verona found herself being guided firmly across the floor towards a door leading into the house. Before she could protest, she was danced through its portals into the empty darkness of a small room.

As soon as her eyes grew accustomed to the dim light she tore herself out of Andreas's grasp and made a dive to escape him, only to be caught round the waist and pinioned to his side.

'No, you don't, *yatáki mou*!' He was breathing heavily, his chest rising and falling perceptibly beneath the light dinner-jacket he wore. 'I don't intend to brawl with you in public. If you've got anything more to say, you can say it here—now—while we're alone!' He stared down at her, his brows furrowed, his eyes expectant.

Verona drew in a deep breath. Temper had increased her pulse-rate to send her warm blood racing to the surface of her skin. She was horribly conscious of the silky crêpe of her dress moulding itself to her tingling breasts, enfolding their outraged outline like a second skin. But Andreas should be left in no doubt what she thought about him and his attitudes.

Loyalty to her friend had prevented her from attempting to discuss Katina's future with the Greek girl's brother before, since to do so would implicate Aunt Irini, but all that had changed now. With Bob Grafton's assertions still ringing in her ears, Verona had been handed the ammunition she wanted, without having to betray Katina's confidences.

'How dare you take me to task for some imaginary flirtation, when what you're proposing to do is infinitely worse?' she snapped. 'Bob told me you planned to arrange a marriage for Katina before you settled down yourself, and I find that despicable. I don't see why she can't live with you and Yana after you're married!'

She saw the shock register on his face before he said icily, 'Can you not? But then, you know nothing of our culture or our customs, it would appear, despite your pretensions to education. And I didn't employ you to listen to vicious gossip, particularly from a man whose sole intent is to avenge himself for what he sees as the wrong I've done him.'

'Precisely!' she stormed triumphantly, grasping the opportunity to make another point. 'Tonight Bob Grafton was seeking vengeance. He assumed, mistakenly, that I was another one of your conquests. I imagine he wanted to give you a taste of your own medicine.' She threw her head back proudly. 'Do you think I enjoy being grabbed and fondled, held and assaulted against my will? Because that's what happened. When Bob Grafton kissed me it was without my consent, and I found it as unwelcome and unpleasurable as when you did the same thing to me the first time we met!'

'And what about the second time, *yatáki mou*?' Andreas almost purred the question, but his hard eyes were brightly accusing. 'Did you find it so unwelcome when you slipped from the rocks and landed in my arms, hmm?'

'More so!' she flung back at him almost without thought. 'Because...' She stopped as a wave of colour flooded her cheeks.

It had been more disquieting, that second embrace, with the sea forcing her lightly clad body into such an intimate contact with Andreas's unyielding frame that she'd been left in no doubt of his desire for her. Of course, she knew such a response was triggered by nature rather than conscious purpose, but the memory of that moment remained to taunt her. Would she ever forget how she'd felt when his body had sought hers...the overriding wish to surrender to him...to let him engulf her with his adamantine power and purpose? She was still ashamed and frightened of the weakness she'd discovered in herself that morning, and the realisation robbed her of words.

'Because you were caught between the devil and the deep blue sea?'

'Two equally threatening forces?' Gratefully she latched on to his explanation, delighted to rationalise her own ambivalent feelings towards the dark-browed Greek who was regarding her with a brooding expression. 'Yes, I suppose you could say that. Ever since I came here you've threatened me without any justification. Tonight you dressed me up like some...some paramour...then left me alone in an alien environment at the mercy of your girlfriend's previous lover! Frankly, if anyone has a case to answer, it's *you*, Andreas—and I consider myself entitled to your apology!'

She was shaking with pent-up emotion as she stopped speaking, uncertain how he'd take her outburst, but relieved to have spoken her mind.

'Do you, indeed?'

The look he gave her was pensive, his face a composed mask hiding his true feelings, but she felt instinctively that she had shaken his complacency by her demand. Staring into her flushed face, one eyebrow slightly raised, the corners of his strong mouth beginning to curve into a vulpine smile, he kept her waiting for a full ten seconds before speaking.

'Very well, then,' he conceded at last. 'I apologise for allowing our host to detain me for so long. I had no idea my absence would cause you so much distress.'

It wasn't quite the apology she'd wanted, but it was better than nothing, she supposed.

'Thank you,' she acknowledged stiffly, beginning to turn away from his wickedly mocking gaze, unable to meet the dancing amusement that lingered there, helplessly aware that he'd treated her complaint facetiously.

'Wait, *yatáki mou*!' The order was low-voiced, but vibrant enough to make her halt and turn slowly to face him. 'You don't escape so easily. I brought you to Crete to occupy and amuse my sister, not to sit in judgement on me or query whatever plans I decide to make on my own or her behalf.'

Aware of the increased rhythm of her heart and the glowing warmth of her body beneath the clinging crêpe of her dress, Verona backed away from his menacing presence, one hand behind her reaching out anxiously for the door-handle.

'I'm her friend,' she declared hotly. 'And I can't stay quiet if I think you're making a big mistake. Kati is warm and loving. She needs...'

'She needs what I am trying to provide for her!' Andreas interrupted with cold deliberation. 'And what is more, I don't intend that you shall worry and upset her with half-truths and ill-founded rumours!'

'According to Bob, half Iraklion knows you're planning to marry Yana Theodaxis as soon as you can shrug off your responsibility towards Kati!' She was crazy standing here bandying words with him, when all she had to do was turn and run from him. But her legs were made of water, hardly supporting her weight, let alone giving her the strength to move.

'Presumably the other half, including Katina, don't!' He took two lazy steps towards her. 'And that is how I intend it shall remain, until such time as I decide to take Katina into my confidence.' He was so close to her now that all thoughts of escape forsook her. 'Whatever you think you know, you repeat it to no one. Your lips are sealed, Verona. Is that understood?'

He was threatening her with every line of his taut body and grim-angled face. Yet how could he stop her if she chose to defy him? It was a bitter irony that she had nothing new to impart to Katina, only that her original fears were correct, although the reasons behind Andreas's plans were not as Irini had thought. Andreas could hardly cut her throat, although, looking at him at that moment, she fancied the thought wasn't far from his mind!

'And if they're not?' she asked pertly, unwilling to give him the assurance he needed without a struggle.

'Why, then I shall have to seal them for you!'

He made the final movement before she even guessed what he was about, drawing her unprepared body into his arms, bending his dark head, his lips seeking her soft, surprised mouth to kiss her with an uncompromising purpose.

For five seconds she resisted the unexpected assault, digging her fingers into his arms, trying vainly to twist her head away from the angry pressure of his marauding mouth. And he *was* angry. There was no doubt about that as his solid body dominated her, pressing her against the unyielding door. If she'd ever needed any proof that everything Katina feared was about to happen, then this was it . . . Andreas demonstrating that he neither asked for nor accepted advice, and that to offer it gratuitously was something one did at one's peril!

Yet, strangely, for all its power the kiss wasn't punitive. Her lips recognised the fact before her brain did, parting of their own volition to welcome a deeper embrace. She didn't even realise how her body had betrayed her until she heard Andreas utter what must have been some oath in his native tongue, before accepting her mindless invitation.

There was no defiance left in her as, heated with a barely restrained passion, Andreas's lips moved from her mouth to scorch the burning skin of her neck, to dwell with ardent caresses on the naked flesh of her shoulder before returning to plunder her mouth anew with a powerful, unrestrained need that sent her senses reeling.

She was trembling, not far from tears when he finally released her, shocked by the ardency of her own nature, knowing she'd accepted his demonstration of passion as a willing participant and disgusted at herself for encouraging his belief she was only too used to playing at games of love.

Tentatively she raised her hand to her mouth, feeling the still throbbing tissue of her lips, experiencing deep within herself a warm coil of unknown longing unwinding.

Swallowing deeply, she strove to regain her composure as Andreas stepped away from her, the expression in his light eyes masked by the fall of eyelids heavily tinged with dark lashes.

'I think it's time we rejoined my sister and our friends before our absence is noted and remarked upon,' he said thickly. 'But first of all, I want your promise to keep Bob Grafton's remarks to yourself. If Kati needs to be told anything, then that information will come from me, when I decide the time is right.'

For a moment Verona hesitated, then shrugged her shoulders. 'All right, but I hope you know what you're doing.'

'I hope so, too.' An odd smile transformed the hard line of his mouth as, head held high, Verona preceded him to the door, standing silently before it, allowing him the courtesy of opening it for her: a duty he performed with a slight, formal inclination of his dark head.

Bestowing a scathing glance on his taciturn face, she swept through, praying that the turbulence of her own thoughts wasn't mirrored on her face.

Damn Andreas for everything he'd done to her! His caustic misjudgements, his arrogantly administered caresses, his stubborn insistence on organising Kati's life—because he certainly hadn't denied her accusation! But he was guilty of a far worse transgression than all those. The appalling truth she could no longer hide from herself, despite every attempt to do so, was that she'd begun to fall in love with him! It was illogical and inexplicable, but it was the only possible explanation for what was happening to her.

She lifted her chin a little higher in mute defiance of her own feelings as she followed Andreas across the dance-floor. She must never let him guess. To do so would place her totally in his power, and for the first time in her life she felt inadequate to deal with such a situation.

Love wasn't only blind, it was unpredictable, she told herself grimly, sinking gracefully into the chair he pulled out for her as they reached their table. Against all reason, she was beginning to care deeply for this beautiful, over-bearing tyrant of a man who was planning to marry another woman, but whose smile could turn her heart even while his scorn ripped her apart.

She knew the symptoms. Hadn't she watched her own mother's transformation as she'd discovered love for the first time? Shivering at the intensity of her own thoughts, Verona lifted her wineglass to take a long, cooling sip. Even while every cell in her brain rebelled against Andreas, every fibre of her being, every beat of her heart, clamoured for his nearness. It was something she had never anticipated happening to her, and she was totally without any defences to combat it. It was a dilemma she must resolve—and quickly.

CHAPTER SIX

IT WAS late when Verona awakened the next morning, stretching luxuriously, screwing her eyes up against the fingers of morning light that stroked her face.

Memories from the previous evening flooded back to her: the way her boredom and disenchantment had vanished the moment she and Andreas had rejoined the small group at the table; the manner in which his command of English had drawn her into the conversation with such skill she could have sworn she was speaking directly to the Liviticos family without need for translation; the exhilaration of dancing with him, held close but not too close, in his strong arms, their bodies perfectly attuned to the changing rhythms.

She stared at the white ceiling. Even her abhorrence of his plans for Katina and the hollow feeling she experienced every time she thought about Yana Theodaxis had failed to obliterate the magic of the evening. What had they talked about? She'd been flying so high, intoxicated by her newly accepted awareness of her feelings towards her imperious partner, that she couldn't recall a word!

Stirring restlessly, still dazed by the unexpected revelation of the true nature of her emotions, she was horrified by what she recognised as a growing need within herself to justify herself to Andreas. An angry little noise of self-disgust escaped her. Up till now she'd always been independent and respected for it. In university she'd shunned the organised women's groups with their vociferous demands for equality. Not because she thought them wrong, but because she'd always been accorded equality without having to fight for it. Her opinions had been listened to, her arguments judged by their virtues, her conclusions given the same consideration as those of her male counterparts.

Her femininity was a fact of life. Something she'd seen no need either to deny or take advantage of. Always she'd dealt person to person with her contemporaries—not woman to man. Until now. Until Andreas.

Furiously she pounded her pillow. From their first meeting he'd seen her only in the guise of her sex and, worse still, he'd typecast her into the stereotyped role of the northern European liberated woman readily open to seduction by the right man... or, worse still, any man!

A sigh escaped her lips. That absurd meeting at the airport hadn't helped matters either, she admitted to herself resignedly. What chance did she have of persuading Andreas that her experience of men was negligible? Especially since her own body had belied her innocence so wantonly in his arms?

The pale blue chiffon of her nightdress drifted to the floor as, swinging her legs out of bed, she removed it to step naked into the vacant shower, her thoughts intent on her predicament.

If it had been only physical attraction she might have been able to cope with this unlooked-for complication. But it was more than that, she admitted wearily to herself. The painful truth was that, even while he antagonised her with his reactionary attitudes, she'd begun to admire his business aptitude, his charisma, the very strength of character that brought them into conflict...

Oh, this was impossible! She turned the shower-spray to cold, gritting her teeth as the cool water bathed her heated skin. Andreas cared nothing for her. As he himself had so succinctly put it, she wasn't one of 'their' women. She was a casual visitor. One of a type with whom the locals amused themselves during the summer before waving them goodbye when the days shortened into autumn.

Stepping from the shower, winding a soft towel round her naked body, Verona forced herself to face the truth. Despite the fact that Andreas had made no attempt to deny an imminent marriage, he still wasn't immune to the physical attractions of other women. The way he had kissed her the previous night had left her in no doubt about that, even if she hadn't had Bob Grafton's assertions to go on!

But the bitter reality was that the passionate kiss which had thrilled her to the border of ecstasy had been born of Andreas's contempt for her and everything she represented to his prejudiced viewpoint.

Deeply troubled, she sighed despondently as she finished drying herself and started to put on a floral-printed towelling beachdress. Since she could no longer hide from herself the fact that she was in love with Andreas, how could she possibly hide it from him? His knowledge would leave her hopelessly vulnerable both to his cruel barbs and his arrogant caresses, and heaven knew where that would lead! This was the last thing she'd expected or wanted! For the first time in her life she was no longer in control of her own destiny. Bob had suggested that many Greek women viewed their menfolk's romantic lapses with equanimity. Even if Yana was one of them, it was no consolation.

Some women could handle a holiday affair, even thrive on it, but not Verona Chatfield, and particularly not when she knew of another woman's involvement, however complacent the latter might be! No one could prevent themselves from falling in love, any more, she thought wryly, than escaping an attack of chicken pox. Hopefully both afflictions were curable.

There remained only one solution. She must leave Crete and return to England while she still had the determination to do so.

Even now, it seemed incredible she could experience such a depth of emotion for a man whose ethics and beliefs were so far removed from her own and whose opinions of her were so low. The only possible way of keeping her self-respect entire was to claim a growing anxiety to resume her career—and bid him a cool and polite farewell.

She would be suffering delusions of grandeur if she imagined for one moment that her opinion could influence Andreas one way or another as far as Katina was concerned. Common sense told her that, since it was obvious Katina was well adjusted to her return to Crete, her brother would no longer insist on her returning to Yorgos and Irini—particularly since he must be anxious to effect the introduction that would leave him free to live his own life.

'Verona—is that you?' Kati's voice drifted across from the other bedroom.

'Uh-huh. How do you feel this morning?'

'Marvellous, fantastic!' The younger girl's voice oozed satisfaction. 'I'm happier now than I've ever been before in my life. Oh, it's so good to be back home and on holiday.' She sighed voluptuously as Verona experienced a sharp stab of guilt.

She mustn't allow herself to be swayed by sentiment, she warned herself. Since she didn't have a hope in hell of changing Andreas's mind, even her loyalty to Katina's interests mustn't distract her from her purpose. She'd be a fool if she continued to expose herself to his potent mixture of charm and disdain, which drew her like a magnet then repulsed her like a sword.

Clearly her friend was no longer the shy, self-effacing teenager she'd first encountered in England. Whatever the traumas of her past, she'd fought and conquered them. Last night the final metamorphosis had occurred. Katina had appeared in public as a beautiful, elegant and accomplished young lady.

Stephanos Liviticos had certainly been aware of it, and Andreas would have had to be blind if he hadn't seen the admiring glances his young sister had drawn from many of the young men present. If anyone was to oppose his plans, then it must be Kati herself. Somehow she would have to find the inner reserves to prevent herself from being manipulated.

It was even possible, Verona accepted sadly, that her own continued presence would make Andreas even more intractable in his decision. No, in the circumstances, Katina's interests too were best served by her departure. But, out of fairness to her friend, Katina must be the first to know. She would tell her—and then she'd break the news to Andreas.

In many respects, she mused as she dressed, it was odd that he hadn't dismissed her out of hand. Probably, she conjectured, he didn't want to distress the younger girl just when his plans were coming to fruition, but it was impossible to foresee a situation where he wouldn't accept her resignation with delight.

However, as the day progressed Verona found it more difficult than she'd hoped to broach Katina on the subject as, try as she might, a feeling of guilt refused to vanish from her conscience. Whereas Katina bustled around the villa singing snatches of popular Greek songs and chattering away without any real purpose, Verona found it hard to concentrate on anything as she accomplished her own small share of the household chores.

By early afternoon, when Katina's buoyant *joie de vivre* had run itself down and she announced her intention of sunbathing on the balcony, Verona wanted nothing more than to get away by herself: to walk in the heat and silence of the Cretan afternoon; to expose her turbulent emotions to the healing atmosphere of the Greek high summer.

Leaving the Greek girl stretched out on a sun-lounger, she changed into shorts and a cotton T-shirt before setting out on one of her favourite walks, climbing towards the mountains that ringed Renagia.

Beneath her feet she could feel the rutted hardness of the baked earth as she took the dusty, twisting road that led from smallholding to smallholding, no wider than a dirt track suitable for donkeys. The sun burnt down unremittingly on her bare head and golden arms, licking at the back of her legs with a fiery tongue. Little puffs of red dust rose from her feet as she walked with an easy balanced gait, deliberately controlling her breathing as the steepness of the path increased and she could feel the pull on her thigh muscles.

Reaching a patch of level ground, she turned to gaze down over the aquamarine bay of sparkling sea. The famed Aegean. To her surprise she felt her eyes mist with tears. Even in so short a time she'd grown to love this country with its harsh beauty. To leave it was going to hurt.

She climbed higher, passing between groves of olive trees before turning again into the pulsating, unshaded

heat of the open track. Here small clumps of thistles
with enormous purple heads hugged the sun-baked edges
of the road and small yellow flowers defied their lack
of water, while prickly undergrowth gave off a sweet,
pungent scent that made the crystal air as heady as wine.
The only sound was the vibrant thrum of cicadas and
the gentle buzz of Cretan honey bees returning to their
isolated hives.

Returning to the villa, Verona was tired, aching in
every limb and dying of thirst. Her legs were covered in
the hot, sandy dust of the mountain tracks, her forehead
beaded with sweat and her hair lying in damp tendrils
against her neck. And she had resolved nothing. She still
felt as miserable and unsettled as when she'd started
out . . . Water first, she decided: a nice long, cool drink,
and then a shower.

She was half-way to the kitchen when Katina whirled
into the room.

'Verona, Verona . . . oh, you'll never guess! It's
Stephanos! It's not a stranger, after all. It's Stephanos
Liviticos Andreas wants me to marry!'

The Greek girl's cheeks were flushed, her eyes
sparkling, her wide smile radiating a vital happiness.

'I'm sorry . . .' Verona pushed a weary hand through
her sweat-dampened hair. The sun couldn't have af-
fected her that badly, surely? 'Do you mean you don't
mind? But Kati, you were horrified when your aunt let
Andreas's plans for you slip out, whatever you said to
me later, here at the villa . . .'

Katina grinned. 'But this is different, don't you see?
I thought it was going to be some elderly business acquaintance of Andreas's, but Stephanos is gorgeous!
He's only a few years older than myself and so good-
looking I can't believe he's interested in me!' She sped

on, not waiting for any comment. 'Just after you left, Andreas arrived and told me. Oh, Verona, you can't imagine how delighted I am...'

Staring speechlessly at her friend, Verona was astonished by what she'd just announced and by the aura of radiance that surrounded her.

'Oh, Verona...I'm so excited!' Katina clasped her hands and performed a little pirouette.

She was like a small child delighted by a birthday present, Verona registered with a sinking feeling in her heart. There was no doubting Katina's happiness, but she was obviously letting relief blind her to what she might be letting herself in for, Verona thought, staring at her aghast.

'That was the first time you'd met Stephanos—at Chigwell Vayne's party?' She couldn't keep the horror from her voice, at what appeared to be the younger girl's unequivocal acceptance of the proposition, after her earlier qualms.

'Oh, no.' Katina's smile widened. 'That's what makes it so marvellous! We used to play together as children and we met several times as teenagers, but then Stephanos went to college and I was at home with Mama. Afterwards he had to do his National Service and Mama died so I was sent to England...'

Her voice, momentarily saddened at the remembrance of her mother's sudden death, rose again excitedly. 'I always liked him. Don't you think he's the most handsome man you've ever seen?'

Recalling the young Greek, Verona had no need to lie. 'Gorgeous,' she agreed with a smile. 'But Kati...you don't really know him. Are you sure it's what you really want?'

'Why not?' Katina was amused. 'Don't you see, Verona, Andreas wasn't trying to cement some business relationship? So he must genuinely like and trust Stephanos or he'd never have agreed to it. There's nothing in it for him—that's why I'm so happy! Stephanos must love me!'

Despite all her good resolutions about not overtly interfering, Verona winced as she thought of Yana Theodaxis. Concerned as she was, nothing would have made her disillusion Katina on precisely where her brother's vested interests lay! Somehow, though, she must introduce a note of caution into her friend's euphoria.

'Your brother isn't the one who's going to have to live with him for the rest of his life,' she told her drily.

Katina smiled complacently. 'Actually they're very much alike in many ways. It's probably why Andreas approves of him and I like him so much.'

Her thirst temporarily forgotten by the shock of her friend's unexpected announcement, Verona regarded the Greek girl's glowing face. Had Andreas suspected that she, Verona, would break the promise he had extorted from her the previous night? Was that the reason for this sudden revelation?

'That's fine as far as it goes,' she suggested gently. 'But the qualities one accepts in a brother aren't necessarily the same one looks for in a husband.'

'No?' Katina seemed surprised. 'Caring, kindness, generosity...'

'Fidelity?' Verona's hazel eyes made no attempt to disguise the deep concern she felt. 'Wouldn't that be important to you as well, Kati? Do you know Stephanos well enough to judge whether he'd be faithful to you?'

'I'm not sure any woman knows that about any man,' Katina replied seriously, in no way abashed by the question. 'But Stephanos wants to marry me, and marriage here in Greece isn't undertaken as lightly as it is elsewhere.' Her young face was thoughtful as she returned Verona's gaze. 'I'm not saying Greek husbands aren't unfaithful, but I am saying it's unimportant, because it's very unusual for a Greek to desert his wife and family for another woman.'

'Oh, Katina!' Verona shook her head in despair, as the Greek girl confirmed Bob Grafton's observation.

She just hadn't anticipated Andreas presenting his plans so speedily and, despite her earlier resolutions of not interfering, she was finding she couldn't stand by silently when she was convinced her friend was being railroaded down a path simply to suit Andreas's convenience.

Drawing in a deep breath, she phrased her question with care. 'You've known him for such a short time, Kati. How can you be so sure he's the right one for you?' she asked softly. 'After all, you haven't had any other boyfriends with whom you can compare him.'

'Which is the reason my sister has such a high market-value!'

Andreas stood looking at her, his expression baleful. Beautifully dressed in a light fawn suit that emphasised the graceful proportions of his magnificent body, straight brows tensed and furrowed over eyes as cold as the peaks of Mount Ida in winter, mouth held in a tight line above a jaw set for trouble, he was a forbidding presence.

Silently cursing her own stupidity in not noticing that his Mercedes was still parked outside, Verona felt her whole tired body grow defensively rigid as she sensed a raw masculinity about Andreas that would be quite im-

pervious to reason. An animal essence that would respond only to the baser qualities of nature—the need to
fight, to win and hold supremacy; a need to conquer
and be acknowledged as a conqueror; and, of course,
an almost megalomaniac wish not to have his orders
questioned.

Once he had demanded of her if she was seeking a
confrontation with him. At the time she had denied it.
Now it seemed inevitable.

'I see Katina's put you in the picture about young
Stephanos's proposal?' He dwelt with disdain on her
exhausted body, making her embarrassingly aware of the
long length of dust-blemished legs she was displaying
beneath her trim action shorts. There was nothing in
that cold gaze to suggest he saw her as anything other
than an unmitigated nuisance.

'I thought it was *your* proposal!' she retorted with
more bravado than she was feeling.

'Did you, now?' He smiled grimly. 'I see I shall have
to have a little talk with you.'

'If you must.' She forced her shoulders into a negligent
shrug. Aware of Katina's worried frown, she didn't want
to enter into a full-scale argument in front of her. 'But
another time, if you don't mind. I'm thirsty and I need
a shower.'

Without waiting for his response, she strode into the
kitchen, taking a tumbler from the open rack and
pouring herself a glassful of cool, refreshing water. She
didn't realise Andreas had followed her until she felt his
hand on her arm and heard his voice, low but intense,
in her ear. 'It's not my intention to parch you into com-
pliance, *yatáki mou*. Water you may have. The shower
can wait.'

'Possibly, but it's not going to!' Verona made to push past him, only to have her arm seized.

'Very well, if you insist.' He moved swiftly towards the stairs, taking her forward with her own momentum. 'I can talk to you just as well upstairs as down here.'

Could he, indeed? She gritted her teeth. This was all she needed—to have him lurking in her bedroom while she was naked under the shower. It was bad enough facing him fully dressed. She had no wish to undergo a tongue-lashing from him without the protection of even her skimpy shorts and cotton top and with only the barrier of the bathroom door between them.

Turning on him sweetly, she batted her eyelashes, much as she'd done at the airport. 'I suppose your sister's used to you going up to shower with your ladyfriends,' she said softly. 'But don't you suppose she'll think it a mite odd if you disappear upstairs with the hired help?'

'Undoubtedly, if she were here.' His other hand rose to grasp her free arm and his smile was no less sweet than her own and just as insincere. 'But while you were refreshing yourself I took the opportunity of sending her out to do a little shopping for me from the beach supermarket. I've told her not to hurry back, and that I'll meet her in half an hour at the taverna next door for a pre-dinner drink.'

His mocking words echoed in the silence as Verona realised with a tingle of dismay that Katina had indeed vanished. Heavens! Now what had she let herself in for? The other girl's presence would at least have kept the conversation on a civilised level. On the other hand, there were several things she wanted to say to Andreas that were better said outside Kati's hearing.

'Very well,' she said sharply, as if he'd given her any real choice. 'As your time is limited I'll postpone my shower.'

'Good.' His mouth curved derisively as she swung away from the stairs, escaping his clutch to make for the sitting-room. Flinging herself into one of armchairs, she flicked him what she hoped was an icy glare as he lowered his long length into a facing chair. Dear God, how was it possible to love *and* resent him at the same time, as she did at that moment?

'Well?' she demanded peremptorily, trying to force out of her mind what had happened the last time she'd had an encounter with Andreas in the same room. Not being entirely successful, she prayed the grim-faced Greek opposite her would dismiss her heightened colour as being sun-induced.

'Well,' he said at length after subjecting her to a thoughtful stare, 'do you really believe I'd agree to anything that isn't in Katina's best interests? Or were you trying to put doubts in her mind just to antagonise me?'

So that was how he wanted to read her genuine affection for his sister! If she'd felt a passing remorse for interfering, it evaporated instantly at his uncompromising attitude.

'I don't accept your right to make plans for another person's life,' she retorted curtly, hating and loving him in equal parts as he thrust his long legs out in front of him.

'I have every right where Katina's concerned!' His jaw tightened angrily.

'Perhaps you forget she's not some little girl from a mountain village, illiterate and fit only to help in the fields and rear children! She's an articulate, highly educated young woman capable of arranging her own future!'

Had she gone too far? A tremor of alarm tightened the skin on Verona's scalp as she deliberately incited his wrath. Yet nothing could have restrained her, so strong was the need to attack everything about him she saw as reactionary and unreasonable.

'And perhaps you don't know she owes *that* fact to me!' Andreas bit back savagely, his temper rising to meet her own, eyes narrowing to an attacking probe. 'Kati's educated because I ensured it: of my own free will and out of my own pocket!'

'And that entitles you to pick a husband for her?' Scorn laced Verona's voice with acid.

'What would you prefer me to do?' Taunting eyes challenged her agitation. 'Suggest she goes out and picks up some boy along the beach or at a disco because she likes the look of his face? Is marriage so unimportant to you that you pay no more attention to how it should be contrived than you would to jumping into a swimming pool?'

'On the contrary,' Verona flared back, glad to be given the opportunity of making her views known, 'I consider it one of the most important decisions a woman can make—but not the only one. There are many women who want more out of life than merely being a man's consort. They need more for fulfilment than their biological duties of child-bearing and rearing can offer them! They need intellectual stimulus and satisfaction as well.'

'As well—or instead of, do you mean?' He waited, dark eyebrows raised for her answer.

'That depends on the individual woman,' she told him firmly. 'At least it should be realised that they *are* individuals, not an identical group with no options.'

'Your own option being to choose a life of intellectual stimulus rather than physical fulfilment, hmm?' His light eyes were sharply enquiring, but she sensed a glimmer of amusement in their clear depths.

'We weren't discussing me,' she retorted a trifle acidly, 'but yes, since you ask, I should feel smothered by total domesticity. There's a whole world out there and I want to discover it for myself. I don't want to be like one of the kittens you keep calling me—knowing only one environment, dependent for my food and well-being on another person's charity, rearing a litter on a regular basis. I want to be free to move around, to travel, to accept challenges...' She stopped, aware that her voice had quickened with the exhilaration of the life she had projected for herself, feeling embarrassed by her own enthusiasm.

There was a twist to his sensuous mouth, a glitter in his compelling eyes as Andreas asked coolly, 'And this is how Katina feels, too?'

'I...' She hesitated, remembering with a sinking feeling what Katina really felt. There'd never been any question of her not wanting marriage and a family as soon as possible, only the initial fear that to please her brother she would have to marry a man she didn't know and might not even like!

'Well?' he insisted. 'Is that what you're telling me?'

'No,' she admitted truthfully. 'I'm trying to tell you that at least she should be given a choice. An opportunity to find out for herself how she does feel.'

Andreas laughed softly at the defiant lift of her chin. 'But isn't that just what she's been given?'

Verona sent him a tentative look. That bland tone was suspect. Was he simply baiting her, or was he giving her views some credence? She would have to give him the benefit of the doubt. At least he was listening to her!

'Not really,' she returned quietly. 'You may have offered her a chance to marry—but you've given her no chance to fall in love with a man of her own choosing.'

A flicker of something touched his eye, then hardened into sarcasm. 'And what do you know of love?' he scorned. 'Is *this* your definition of it?' To Verona's horror, he reached behind him to produce Katina's copy of *Admissions of Aphrodite*, tossing it into her lap where its powerful arrival stung the bare flesh of her thigh. 'Drifting from one man's arms to another's; one man's bed to another's? Is that how you think my sister should select a mate?'

'Of course not,' she acknowledged shakily. Thank God he didn't realise to whom the book truly belonged. 'But she should be given an opportunity of knowing the man you've chosen for her.' Defiance in every line of her tense body, she met his stern face without balking.

His eyes narrowed on her, cool and enigmatic. 'I can assure you Stephanos's social and economic backgrounds are flawless.' It was almost as if he enjoyed provoking her with his attitude of casual command as he continued, 'His father's company owns several hotels and Stephanos will be accepted on the board when he completes his present training. Katina will be the wife of a respected and wealthy man, with all the security and comfort that suggests. A list of criteria which surely makes him very lovable in most women's eyes, *ne*?'

'Eligible, not lovable,' Verona amended, stung by his cynicism.

'Besides which,' he continued smoothly, ignoring her interruption, 'if it hadn't been for your own interference in my affairs, I'd had every intention of encouraging Katina to know Stephanos better before allowing him to approach her—although they're hardly strangers at the moment, and it was clear last night to everyone who observed them that she is very attracted to him.

'However, since I couldn't rely on your holding your own counsel, I decided to act immediately. Even then, you can't believe I shall have her married within the week?' Dark eyebrows lifted enquiringly, demanding an answer.

To be honest, she didn't know what she'd thought. Katina's announcement, coming out of the blue when she was immersed in her own problems of returning to England, had knocked her sideways. The Greek girl had made the whole thing sound like a *fait accompli* and, the truth was, she wouldn't have put it past Andreas to have made it exactly that!

'I'd no idea what plans you'd made,' she returned at last, refusing to be cowed by the censure darkening his mocking eyes.

'Precisely.' The dark head nodded in satisfaction. 'If you'd been here when I arrived rather than indulging the quirks of your nationality by walking bare-headed in the sun, you might have been better informed.' Verona eyed him warily as he rose to his feet to stand over her. 'By *Theo*, Verona, don't you think I realise Katina is still a child in many ways?' He heaved an impatient breath. 'While Kati was in England, Stephanos came to me and asked my permission to court her. They'd known each other since childhood and it appears he'd been falling in love with her for some time. When she was living with Mama she wasn't encouraged to bring friends home, then the army separated them for two years, but all that time Stephanos remained steady in his purpose.'

He paused for a few moments, thrusting his hands into his trouser pockets with angry impatience. 'What was I to do? I knew and liked Stephanos and his family. On paper he would make an ideal husband for her, but she was young and inexperienced and probably not mature enough to make a rational decision! I suspected, too, she felt under an obligation to me and would do what she imagined I wanted her to!'

So Andreas was not insensitive to Katina's emotional needs and prejudices. Verona returned his steady gaze, but stayed silent. Had he really only acted in Katina's interests? A warm glow of hope began to raise her spirits, as he went on.

'I felt my sister needed a mature person of her own sex in whom to confide at such a time, an older and wiser woman who loved her: someone who would take Mama's place in her life and advise her if she had any doubts.' His dark gaze searched her sunkissed face. 'So I told my Aunt Irini what had transpired, swore her to secrecy and begged her to come here with Kati. Instead...' He shrugged his shoulders.

'Instead you got me,' Verona finished his sentence with a self-deprecating twist of her lips. No wonder he'd been so furious with her, especially after that ridiculous episode at the airport. Instead of the sober, practical middle-aged matron he'd wanted, he'd been faced with the possibility that his sister was going to be led astray and ill advised by some fast-living, amoral tourist!

'Yes,' he agreed softly. 'I got you. Don't spoil it for her, Verona. Don't take this opportunity away from her unless you're very sure you can give her something to replace it.' His voice deepened. 'My sister isn't being forced to marry Stephanos. Decidedly such a union would have my blessing. I've known him all his life and I trust him. He's an honourable and honest young man and I believe he loves Kati. But the final decision must and will be hers.' The fabulous blue eyes were a compelling power as they commanded her attention. 'As you saw, she was thrilled when I told her, but she cares deeply for you and your opinions. Maybe you can talk her out of it with your clever arguments and theories of equality and job satisfaction and a woman's right to determine her own future. That is a risk I'm prepared to take, but if you do...'

'Yes?' Her throat was so dry, Verona could hardly speak.

'Remember that it's a big responsibility to deprive a Greek woman of the chance to enjoy the security of marriage and the feel of her babies' arms round her neck.'

'Not all women want husbands and babies!' She was being forced to speak in clichés, knowing she wasn't acquitting either herself or her beliefs to their advantage. If only the man sitting opposite her didn't arouse these feelings of conflict within her! Verona pushed angry fingers through her hair, releasing some of the pent-up tension that held her body in thrall.

'But all real women want to belong to a man.' He was regarding her stormy, dust-stained face with infuriating superiority. 'And here, in Greece, for most women that still only happens within marriage.'

Unable to meet the probing impertinence of that look, Verona turned her head away, resting her cheek against the soft upholstery, while a sigh of utter despair at her inability to discuss things rationally with him escaped her lips.

In seconds, before her startled limbs had a chance to resist, she found herself pulled to her feet, the instinctive cry of protest that rose in her throat aborted as Andreas plundered her mouth with a kiss both merciless and savage.

Violently angry at the abrupt assault on her senses, Verona twisted her body against the confining power of his arms in a vain attempt to free herself.

Even while she struggled, she knew what was happening to her. She could feel her breasts swell and harden in response to his nearness, the warmth of his flesh against hers, the brush of his skin and the element of uncontrolled anger than ran like a thread through all his actions.

She felt her eyes fill with unwilling tears. How was it possible for a man to despise a woman as Andreas obviously despised her and still want this? The answer didn't bear thinking about.

When he released her mouth with the abruptness with which it had been captured, gasping with a strange mixture of shame and desire, Verona closed her eyes, praying he wouldn't see their dampness, unable to prevent a low moan of despair as Andreas moved one unhampered hand over her taut breasts, brushing their fullness with reverent fingers.

'You see,' he told her with quiet satisfaction. 'You are all woman, *yatáki mou*. You, too, need to belong to a man.'

'No...' Her hoarse denial rejected not only his insolent diagnosis but everything he'd subjected her to within the preceding minutes.

His hand dropped from her breast, but he remained standing before her, so close she could feel the sweet, warm breath from his mouth caress her cheek and hear the increased effort of his breathing as it laboured within the strongly developed confines of his hard chest.

Conscious of the piercing, unsmiling regard from his heavily lidded eyes, Verona sought desperately to announce her decision to escape from his oppressive authority.

How dared he assume she would try to push hardline feminist views down his sister's throat when all she wanted was to prevent Katina making a rash decision without considering what she was about to do?

The angry words of resignation were actually trembling on her lips when she hesitated. Wouldn't it seem she'd allowed herself to be cowed by his lecture, almost an admission that she was as shallow and promiscuous as he judged her?

She heaved a deep breath, trying to control the nerves that brought cool tremors to her skin. Suppose Katina did have second thoughts about marrying Stephanos in the coming weeks? Wouldn't she need some moral support before she could face her autocratic brother with a decision that would destroy his carefully laid plans? For, despite Andreas's explanation, the fact still remained that Kati's marriage was very much in her brother's interests!

'Have your shower, Verona. You look as if you need it. Then we'll go and join Katina.'

His dismissal was absolute. Only for a few seconds did she consider trying to sustain the discussion before logic told her it would achieve nothing. In these circumstances, discretion was definitely the better part of valour. Silently she made her retreat.

CHAPTER SEVEN

SHIFTING her body gingerly on the hard concrete surround of the Olympic-sized swimming pool in the grounds of the nearby hotel, Verona admitted ruefully that it wasn't the ideal place to sunbathe. Unfortunately for her comfort, all the sunloungers had been purloined by the hotel guests.

Normally she would have stretched out on the sandy beach between the hotel and the road leading to the villa, but Sunday was family day, the narrow fringe of sand packed with vociferous groups of Greek families enjoying themselves.

Previously she'd delighted in sharing their pleasure, enjoying the sight of elderly grandmothers dressed in black, dark-haired, voluptuous mothers and sloe-eyed children relaxed and happy on their day of rest. It had seldom failed to touch her watching the proud Greek fathers, bronzed and muscular, cavorting with their offspring while the majority of the women took a more leisurely look at life.

Today the scene on the beach served only to remind her of Andreas's traditionalism. So instead she'd escaped to this haven of tourism, amusing herself by watching the antics of the *kamaki* as they strutted and preened in front of the lissom blonde Swedish and German girls.

A pang of hunger reminded her she hadn't eaten since lunch the previous day, having been too confused and upset to join Andreas and Katina for dinner. Since she was still nursing the pain his mocking assessment of her character had inflicted, it would have been unbearable to share a table with him. Fortunately, it hadn't been necessary to look far for an acceptable excuse.

'You and Katina will have a lot to discuss,' she'd told him after having showered and re-dressed herself in a cool dress of rainbow-coloured voile. 'My presence would only be intrusive in the circumstances.'

Much to her relief, he'd accepted her reason as valid, enabling her to spend the evening wrestling alone with the effects of her unruly passions!

Lazily she rose to her feet. Since Katina had left Renagia early that morning for Iraklion in response to a peremptory summons from her brother, she had only herself to cater for. There was bread and the delicious *graviera* cheese in the fridge, plus plenty of fresh salad and a ripe melon, so she might as well start walking slowly back there.

Gathering her towel, she stowed it away in her beach-bag, making her way down through the lush gardens of the hotel to where a flight of stone steps led directly to the main beach. Weaving her way through the sun-bathers spreadeagled beneath the azure sky, she reached the water's edge, allowing the warm eddy of the sea to caress her bare feet as she started towards her destination.

So intent was she on avoiding the children running in and out of the shallows that she nearly jumped a foot in the air when an arm encircled her swimsuit-clad waist from behind.

'Ah! It seems I haven't had a wasted journey, after all!'

'Bob!' Surprise and annoyance were finely balanced in her reaction as Verona recognised her assailant. 'I don't know how you've the nerve to speak to me again, or...' she added as an afterthought '...how you even knew where to find me!'

Bob Grafton swung into step beside her as she disengaged herself from his grasp.

'I made it my business to find out all the places Yana was likely to be spending her days—and nights.' His frown was transient, replaced almost instantly by the charming smile she remembered from their first meeting. 'And as for daring to speak to you again, I've come to give you the opportunity of slapping my face...as I deserve.'

'Yes, you do, don't you?' Verona found it impossible to remain angry with him in the face of such disarming frankness. Deliberately she thrust from her mind his allusion to Yana and the unwelcome pictures it had instantly conjured. She turned an accusing gaze on him. 'You saw Andreas Constanidou approaching and deliberately set me up!'

'No, my love.' He shook his tawny head. 'I set myself up. I knew he'd resent my touching any woman he'd laid a claim to, and I needed to see for myself how strong his commitment to you was.'

'There's no commitment,' Verona said coldly.

He ignored her protestation. 'The more I thought about the way he marched you away, the more worried I got for your well-being.' He slid her a sideways glance. 'If what I did made trouble between you—then I'll willingly tell him you had no part in it.'

Verona shrugged uninterested shoulders. 'You're indulging in wishful thinking, I'm afraid. There's nothing personal between us. If Andreas was annoyed at what happened, it was because he thought I was setting Kati a bad example. That's all.'

'Hmm.' Bob cast perceptive eyes over her still face. 'You certainly don't bear any physical signs of his displeasure, at least not where they show!' He ran his thoughtful gaze over the exposed skin of her shoulders and legs.

'You didn't think he was going to beat me!' Laughter welled in her throat at such an incredible thought. 'He may be a bit autocratic, but he's hardly a brute!'

'You'd be surprised what jealousy can do even to the most civilised of men.' Naked, tanned shoulders moved wearily. 'Look at me. Who would have thought a few months ago I'd be eating my heart out for a woman—especially one who walked off with another man—prepared to go anywhere, do anything to get her back!'

There was pity on Verona's face as Bob kicked despairingly at the water.

'But I thought you said it was too late—that she was going to marry Andreas...' Had he been guessing? she wondered, a tiny thrill of expectation running through her.

'Oh, that's the plan, all right,' he returned bitterly. 'I got it from the horse's mouth, so to speak. But in my book it's never too late until the contract's been signed.'

'You've seen Andreas?' Verona fell into step beside him as he began to walk slowly along the water's edge. 'He actually admitted it to you?'

He nodded. 'I saw them both yesterday morning having coffee in Lion Square in Iraklion. Imagine, for months I've been trying to get in touch with Yana, and suddenly there she is as large as life!' He gave a bitter laugh. 'So I waited until Constanidou went inside to pay the bill, then I went up to her.'

'And?' She could hardly conceal her anxiety.

'She wouldn't even listen to what I wanted to say. She told me everything was over between us, that she and Constanidou were getting married just as soon as he'd sorted out his domestic arrangements. Hell!' he blurted out explosively. 'We lived together as lovers for two years. I really thought there was too much between us for another man to break us up.' Grim lines bisected his cheeks. 'I haven't given up yet, though. What I need is to see her somewhere privately and alone—not in the middle of a crowded square with everyone gawping at us.' He gave Verona a sideways glance. 'That's the second reason I've come here this morning. To ask you if you've any idea where he's keeping her—I mean, has he let any clue slip?'

'No, none.' Verona shook her blonde head. Dear heavens, she didn't want to act the part of an agony aunt at the moment. Neither was she at all sure that she would have given Bob the information he wanted even if she had known. Yana was a free agent and didn't deserve to be harassed. 'Domestic arrangements', she had said. That could only mean when Andreas had seen his sister safely married to Stephanos!

She stumbled suddenly on the warm sand, toppling against Bob's body, accepting his restraining hand gratefully as he prevented her from falling.

'Whoa...' He slanted her an understanding smile, momentarily jerked out of his own self-pity. 'Too much sun, by the look of it.' He gestured to one of the many tavernas ringing the beach. 'Come on, I'll buy you lunch to prove my penitence. Who knows, while we're eating you might recall some hint as to where Yana's hiding out.'

Wordlessly Verona allowed him to lead her into the cool vine-shaded restaurant, subsiding into a chair with a sigh of relief. There was nothing to remember, but her legs felt like jelly and there were beads of perspiration on her forehead. It would be sensible to eat.

Presumably Bob had left Yana in Lion Square before Andreas had returned. But had Yana recounted the meeting? Almost certainly, Verona decided. Had that been the reason for Andreas's urgent morning phone call summonsing his sister to Iraklion? Was he about to tell her of his impending wedding? Despite everything he'd said, did he mean to exert this subtle form of blackmail over Katina, implicitly suggesting that if she turned Stephanos down there might no longer be a home for her in Crete?

A knife twisted in Verona's heart. Last night she had wanted to believe he truly had the welfare of his sister at heart, that he wanted the best for the young girl who'd been so tragically deprived of a father and unnaturally confined to the side of a sick mother.

Perhaps Stephanos Liviticos *was* everything Andreas claimed him to be. But would it have mattered, anyway? Verona gnawed at the problem while Bob glanced through the stereotyped menu common to all beachside tavernas. On the surface it would be a good marriage. Good enough in practical terms to salve Andreas's conscience if all he needed was to shed responsibility for Kati.

Had Stephanos really approached him as he'd claimed, or had he engineered the whole thing...?

'Where is the delectable Katina today, anyway?' Bob asked, handing the menu across the table.

Verona laid it down unseeingly. 'Andreas asked her to meet him at his apartment in Iraklion this morning.' She stared down at the tablecloth. 'She went in by cab.'

She hadn't questioned the reason, and Katina had been far too excited to discuss the summons, rushing around changing her casual clothes for something smarter, her eyes glowing with an unspoken happiness as she twisted and turned in front of the mirror. What a tragedy if so much joy should turn out to be the precursor of tragedy.

'It must be my lucky day to find you alone.' Bob tossed her a friendly smile, which didn't reach his eyes. 'Have you decided what you want to eat?'

Tearing her mind away from Katina's problems, Verona chose prawns in cheese batter with an accompanying salad and settled down to get what enjoyment from the situation she could.

To do him justice, Bob Grafton was an amusing companion, and she was glad not to have to suffer her own solitary state. It was while they were having a second cup of coffee and Bob was downing a large Metaxa that she thought to ask him about the film script.

'Hercules, you mean?' His mouth twitched in self-mockery. 'Settled at last. Strictly between you and me, he's been turned into a duodecathlete.'

'A what?' She voiced her amazement.

'Duodecathlete,' Bob repeated patiently. 'A decathlete plus two! The twelve labours of Hercules, see?'

'Oh! I like it!' Verona laughed in genuine delight, clapping her hands in approbation. 'Dare I ask what two disciplines you've added?'

'Boxing and swimming,' Bob answered smugly. 'That way we get to milk it dry—a combination of *Jaws*, *Chariots of Fire* and *Rocky*. Clever, eh?'

'Brilliant!'

They were both laughing, flushed with wine and the pleasure of instant comradeship, when the shadow fell squarely over the table.

'It sounds a good joke,' Andreas said quietly. 'Am I allowed to share it?'

'Constanidou.' Bob acknowledged his presence with a sharp nod of his tawny head, leaning back nonchalantly to survey the dark, unsmiling face of the Greek with a casual uninterest which reeked of impertinence.

Verona's fingers curled into her palms as she scented the danger sparking in the sombre, heavily lidded eyes that turned to sweep their regard across the tanned expanse of skin above the delicate nylon satin of her emerald swimsuit.

Horribly aware that her nipples were proudly prominent beneath the taut covering, partly because it was the way she was made, partly because beneath the close vines the air was pleasantly cool, and partly for reasons she didn't care to consider, she swallowed deeply.

'I came to take you out to lunch.' His pleasant voice was controlled, almost casual. 'But I see I'm a little too late.'

'In more ways than one.' The lazy taunt from Bob's maliciously curving lips was appallingly suggestive. Furious with him, Verona felt the hot blood colour her cheeks.

'Really?' Superbly relaxed, hands thrust deep into pockets of light, closely tailored trousers, a spotless white cotton shirt stretched across smoothly rounded pectorals, Andreas gazed down with obvious condescension at Bob's naked torso, his tongue thoughtfully caressing the long, sweet bow of his upper lip. 'I'd suggest you go back to Iraklion and mind your own affairs instead of meddling with mine.'

'So Verona *is* your affair!' Bob pushed his chair away, rising angrily to his feet. 'That's just what I wanted to hear you admit, Constanidou. And what does Yana think of that—or hasn't she found out yet?'

Verona saw with a sinking heart the sinews of his bare arms trembling, and knew it had nothing to do with nerves and everything to do with the increased adrenalin flow that precedes action.

'My affairs are my own concern—and no one else's.' Andreas's reply was slow, deeply voiced, deceptively controlled, but Verona wasn't deceived. Inside that beautifully balanced frame was a core of retribution swelling to fruition. If Bob was unaware of it, she most definitely wasn't! At any moment there was going to be an almighty punch-up, and part of the shame of that was going to be hers because she was with them!

'Suppose I want to make them mine?' Bob's chin lifted aggressively as his fist balled. Andreas, the taller and heavier and probably the fitter, didn't miss the signs. His blue eyes gleamed with devilish delight as his shoulders flexed.

'Try it,' he suggested with muted glee.

It was too much! Instantly Verona was on her feet, slapping her hand down on the table to demand their attention, speaking furiously but softly as she achieved her aim.

'I'm not surprised to hear *you* sound like someone in a B-grade movie,' she stormed at Bob, watching the flicker of amazement take the venom from his gaze. 'But *you*...' Putting every nuance of disdain into the words her shaking voice was capable of finding, her eyes met the glazed expression of the tall Greek. 'But you! I doubt if brawling in a bar is likely to endear you to your prospective brother-in-law or impress the sister whose welfare you claim such interest in! And I certainly don't intend staying to watch you both make fools of yourselves!'

It wasn't easy making a dignified exit wearing only a swimsuit. Thank heaven her neat, elegant bottom and long, shapely legs were sufficiently attractive not to be the objects for raucous comments from any observers of her hasty retreat as she flounced down the steps to the beach! Immediately she felt ashamed of her vanity.

Holding her head high, she strode with defiant speed between the groups of Greeks lounging in the sun as she made for the far end of the bay and the sanctuary of the villa.

Dear God! Not only had she dared to stand up to Andreas in public, but she'd let slip by implication his marriage plans for Katina. That wouldn't please him one iota. Still, she thought, striving to find a grain of comfort, she hadn't heard any signs of fracas following her departure. She'd have to hope that reason had prevailed. Not that there wouldn't have been some satisfaction from seeing Andreas with a black eye! Unfortunately she didn't reckon Bob's prowess against Katina's brother in a fight. It wasn't that she held much sympathy for the irritating scriptwriter with his innuendoes, either; it was just that she felt even less for Andreas. Wasn't it sufficient he'd won the other man's woman, without baiting him about it?

'Kati?' Reaching the villa she called her friend's name. As Andreas was back in Renagia then Kati would be too, and the sooner she put the younger girl in the picture about recent events the better. It was all very well for Andreas to say he didn't want his sister to sense any antagonism between the two of them, but after her outburst she doubted if he'd be prepared to hide his feelings towards her...

'Kati?'

But every room was empty. The villa deserted. Of course, the beach supermarkets were open all hours seven days a week. Kati had probably gone out to buy something. There was no need to imagine anything sinister about her absence.

Unexpectedly Verona shivered. Perhaps her swimsuit hadn't dried out as completely as she'd thought. Making her way to her bedroom, she pushed the clinging nylon satin down her body, surprised to find her teeth were chattering.

Nerves? But she wasn't afraid of the dark-browed Greek, was she? No, she assured herself, she was reacting like this because normally she stood back and observed in the true scientific manner. She didn't thrust herself forward into the turmoil of conflict. Yet ever since she'd arrived in Crete she seemed to have been at war with Andreas, and the experience was beginning to tell. What she needed was a nice warm shower to restore her equilibrium.

She'd just finished patting herself dry when she heard the knock on the bedroom door. Useless to pretend she wasn't there—or asleep. Andreas must have heard the sound of the shower, perhaps had deliberately waited until he heard it stop and guessed her to be refreshed and decently clad.

The first she was, but, because she'd spent time in washing her hair... she was certainly as far from decent as it was possible to get.

'Just a moment...' Hastily she reached for the négligé coat that was part of the elegant set her mother had bought her last Christmas. Styled in heavy opaque turquoise satin, cut on tailored lines, it was more like a housecoat than an item of lingerie, concealing her warm curves from throat to heel.

Her fingers shook as she knotted the sash firmly round her waist. God knew she'd got herself in this impossible situation—neither guest nor real employee, and certainly not friend! One thing was certain: she wouldn't take a drachma from Andreas for her so-called services. She'd even repay the air fare as soon as she possibly could. Damn him for looking as he did and for behaving as he did! He ought to have a notice hung round his neck warning unwary women of the havoc he could wreak ... 'This man can seriously damage your health!'

There was a grim smile playing about her lips as she opened the door, guessing that her own health was gravely in jeopardy, to find Andreas standing patiently outside with nothing in his expression to betray his present mood.

'May I come in?'

Suspecting the question was rhetorical, Verona shrugged her shoulders. 'Why not? It's your house.'

'Indisputably.' The lazy tone of his voice matched the measured tread with which he entered. 'But your room, as long as you remain under its roof.' One quick look encompassed her flushed face devoid of make-up and the drying tendrils of spiralling curls that hung to the satin shoulders of her gown before he wandered leisurely across to the window to stand contemplating the luxuriant foliage of a pomegranate tree in the garden beneath.

Staring at his broad-shouldered back with its neat waist and long, smartly trousered legs, Verona forced herself to stay silent. If he was waiting for an apology, he'd stand there all night! She'd just begun to question the advisability of *that* possibility when Andreas himself broke the pulsating silence between them.

'Stephanos came to see me in Iraklion this morning.' The deeply modulated voice showed no emotion. 'In two weeks' time he has to go to Athens on a management training course. As you can imagine, he was very anxious to hear how Katina had reacted to his proposal and, if it was favourable, to invite her down to his family's villa at Aghios Nicolaos from now until he has to leave Crete.'

'And of course you were delighted to encourage her to go...' Verona was surprised at the bitterness in her tone as the reason for Katina's absence became apparent. If Andreas had contrived the invitation himself it couldn't have been more convenient. Here was the perfect excuse for him to rid himself of the bad influence he feared she might assert over his malleable sister, without alienating the younger girl.

'Yes.' He made no attempt to contradict her, turning to regard her with a long, thoughtful stare that made her super-conscious of the fright she must look with her mass of blonde hair billowing round her shoulders, unkempt like a lion's mane. Only there was only one king of the jungle in this room... and it wasn't her!

A wicked smile filled Andreas's eyes with devilment. 'At first Kati was very loath to leave you, but happily I was able to persuade her that it was you who had actually suggested she needed an opportunity to get to know Stephanos better before she committed herself.' The smile deepened. 'I'm sure you agree that to spend two weeks in his company will give her a fair insight into her prospective husband's character, hmm?'

'Yes, indeed,' she agreed crisply. In fact it *was* a good idea, she admitted inwardly. Her original pique at its announcement had been caused by Andreas's taking the initiative in dismissing her when she would have preferred to be the one to resign, but there was nothing she could do about that now. 'I'm just sorry I didn't have the opportunity of saying goodbye to her.' Hazel eyes dared him to deny she had a right to that at least.

'Stephanos was in a hurry to drive back to Aghios Nicolaos. He'd spent the night in Iraklion and there were important matters awaiting his attention. They'd hoped to see you when they called in here to collect Kati's luggage, but . . .' An eloquent shrug. 'It seems you'd already made your own plans for the day, no doubt believing you wouldn't be interrupted.'

Verona caught her breath at the cool allusion to her lunch with Bob Grafton and the inference accorded to it, determining not to dignify his suspicions with an explanation. Instead she said coolly, 'Well, you must give her my love and best wishes for her future, and tell her I'll write when I get back to England.'

Beneath his steady gaze, she slid open the wardrobe door, pulling out her large suitcase. Haphazardly, her eyes misted with tears, she lifted a pile of cotton tops and put them inside.

'Running away?'

Two strong hands imprisoned her wrists as Andreas loomed up behind her, pinioning her arms to her sides and pulling her against the hard musculature of his own body, forcing a gasp of shock from her startled lips. Too conscious of the heavy, angry thud of her own heart and the pounding of enraged blood in her ears, she hadn't heard him move. Twisting furiously, she gazed up into his dark-browed face.

'Leaving!' she told him tautly, controlling her ragged breathing with an effort. 'If you'll phone the airport for me, there's bound to be a seat free on a charter flight.'

It wasn't easy talking with her neck screwed round at an angle and with Andreas's unsmiling face only inches from her own, but she persevered, determined to have her say while he allowed it. 'It's glaringly obvious that Kati no longer needs a chaperon, and there's nothing else to keep me here!'

'Nothing? Are you quite sure about that?'

She was spun round and found herself deposited on the bed. Shaken but unhurt, she gazed with rage-darkened eyes up into Andreas's baleful stare as he towered over her.

'What do I have to do to convince you that Katina's interests are my only motivation?' he demanded thickly.

It was a good question, and he'd never know how desperately she wanted to believe in his altruism or how difficult she was finding it, torn between her own wishful thinking and what she'd learned from Bob Grafton.

'There's nothing you can do,' she answered levelly. 'And there's no reason why you should want to try.'

'Perhaps not,' he agreed shortly. 'But when you accepted this assignment I expected you to see it through.'

'But it's already through, isn't it?' Verona pushed her hand through her hair with impatient irritation. 'Katina's been delivered to her future husband and you're free to do whatever you wish. I just hope for your sister's sake, your motives *are* as honourable as you want me to believe!'

'You dare to question them?' The raw anger underlying Andreas's tone made her shudder, but, far from cowing her, it drove her forward to attack.

'I believe you may be influenced by more than one consideration, yes!' She glared at him. 'After all, Katina's very young. If you weren't contemplating marriage yourself I can't believe you'd be so keen to get her off your hands!'

'Verona!' Her name was a harsh epithet on his tongue as he lunged towards her.

'Don't touch me!' She wrenched herself away from his reaching arms, despising the innermost clamour of her being which longed to respond to his touch.

'Panagia mou!' he swore brutally but softly. 'You're little more than a child yourself.'

His intent look absorbed her fair hair, the golden-tipped lashes devoid of mascara, the faint covering of freckles across her shapely nose. 'Stephanos is an intelligent, cultured man, youthful and healthy, who is wealthy enough to see she wants for nothing. As I told you before, his father owns a chain of hotels throughout Europe, and in time Stephanos will take his place on the board. If Katina wishes to use her education and languages in helping him, she will have plenty of opportunity!'

His lustrous eyes narrowed as she made no answer. 'The fact that I've met a woman I want to marry has nothing to do with it. When Stephanos first approached me I had no intention of becoming a bridegroom! Or,' his brow darkened threateningly as he appeared to read her thoughts, 'perhaps you even doubt Stephanos came to me. What is going on in that golden head of yours, hmm? Do you think I bribed him or blackmailed him somehow to take Katina off my hands?' His voice deepened ominously, increasing in insistence as a frown furrowed the smooth skin of his forehead. 'Well, *yatáki mou*, do you?'

Of course she wanted to believe him. For Katina's sake, but for her own as well. She wanted . . . no, *needed* . . . to believe his integrity as a justification of her own ambivalent feelings towards him.

'No...' She forced herself to meet his smouldering gaze as she accepted his avowal of acting in Katina's best interest.

'Ah...' He expelled his breath in a sigh, as if her good opinion of him had been of the utmost importance. 'Then you'll stay here until she returns, to satisfy yourself she knows her own mind?' Unable to speak because of a sudden unbidden lump constricting her throat, Verona shrugged her shoulders as he continued evenly, 'Two weeks, Verona, that's all, then Kati will be back here with you and you'll have the rest of your stay to satisfy yourself she's happy about marrying Stephanos.'

'And if she's not?'

She'd expected Andreas to dismiss that possibility out of hand, and was surprised when he pursed his lips thoughtfully.

'Then—if Katina won't tell me so herself, *you* will.'

'And—and if that should happen?' Her tawny eyes challenged him.

'Why, then I shall reaffirm to my sister that my only concern is her happiness and that whatever decision she makes is all right with me.' His fingers tightened almost imperceptibly on her shoulders. 'Well?' he demanded impatiently. 'Do we have an agreement?'

Hopelessly entrapped, Verona sought her conscience for an answer. If she stayed she was forcing herself to exist in the presence of a man who held a deadly attraction for her, but whose love was already in the keeping of another woman—a situation which could only hold heartbreak for her. On the other hand, if she chose to leave she would be denying Katina the support that even Andreas acknowledged she might need. Of the two of them, Katina and herself, who was the best able to cope with emotional problems? She was left with only one answer.

'I'll stay until she returns, if that's what you really want.'

'Yes, it is.' Light eyes flickered perceptively over her robed body before returning masked now with amusement to her face. 'And so you won't feel lonely left here alone, or feel obliged to make unsuitable friends, I've already promised Katina I'll take two weeks' holiday and spend the time with you.'

'What?' She couldn't have heard him correctly, as he made his way leisurely towards the door. This was certainly something she hadn't bargained for! As the blood thrummed anew through her veins at the prospect of sharing the villa with him, she prevented his leaving by grabbing out and fastening her hand round his upper arm.

'You mean you intend to stay here at the villa with me—just the two of us?' The words tumbled out furiously. How could she possibly submit to such a bizarre proposition? And how dared he talk about her making unsuitable friends when what he was suggesting was highly unsuitable?

Fuming, she awaited his response, but his face showed only mild interest at her shocked expression, his cool reception only serving to increase her frustration. He could hardly have made it much clearer how low his opinion of her remained! She would just have liked to have seen his reaction if a male acquaintance of Katina's had suggested spending two weeks alone with her in the villa! Whatever his intentions—and they might be quite innocuous—for him to voice them and for her to accept them would be to welcome his further contempt of her life-style as he saw it.

'And what will Yana think of such an arrangement?' she asked tartly, deciding cynicism was the best approach.

'Yana?' He sounded surprised that she should even consider his fiancée's feelings. 'Oh, Yana will understand perfectly.' The complacent smile he turned on her was obviously meant to be reassuring. Instead it drove Verona's blood-pressure up a further two points, as he continued, 'Being Greek, she's well aware of our unwritten laws of hospitality which demand that, having been invited to my country and my house, you cannot now be deserted.' A slight pause before a new note of grimness deepened his steady tone. 'She will also understand that Bob Grafton, under the impression he has a score to settle with me, might take it upon himself to try and seduce you if you are left unprotected.'

This must be how a trapped animal felt! She couldn't, wouldn't spend the next two weeks living in the same villa as Andreas Constanidou! Even his admitted love for Yana Theodaxis didn't convince her that he wouldn't take a perverted pleasure in subjecting her to casual and punitive embraces if the fancy took him, unaware of her true character and the real nature of her feelings towards him.

'That's very considerate of you.' Her eyes sparkled dangerously as she met his bland appraisal, loving and hating united in a dangerous passion. 'But I'm well able to defend myself.'

'Are you?' Black eyebrows rose to question her ability, as she fumed quietly at his studied nonchalance. 'You've a short memory, *yatáki mou*. Not so long ago you demanded an apology from me because I left you alone in an alien environment at the mercy of my girlfriend's lover—remember?'

Verona bit her lip. Of course she remembered the unwilling apology she'd dragged from him on that occasion, and what he'd taken in return.

'I see you do.' His smile was infuriatingly smug. 'If I have one virtue, it's avoiding repeating the same mistake. So—you will stay because you've agreed to do so, and I shall stay here with you because your safety is my responsibility.'

'And who will protect me from you?' It was a trite question, but she couldn't think of another way of putting it, and it was something that had to be asked and answered if she were to have any peace of mind at all.

A smile tugged the corners of his mouth as he surveyed her defiant face, but his eyes were cool and watchful as they met her haughty gaze.

'My promise will protect you,' he told her quietly. 'My promise that I will never do anything with you or to you that offends you. My promise that I mean to spend the next few days making your stay in Crete a memorable one, so that in years to come you will look back on it with pleasure. Is that enough?'

It was a generous statement of intent in the circumstances, and if she hadn't experienced the way her heart leapt at his nearness or felt its heavy pounding when he kissed her, or known her legs go weak when his strong arms cradled her against his vital, masculine body—it might have been enough.

Verona realised she was still holding his arm, and let her hand fall away as if it had been burned. 'There have been times when you've misread my reactions to your—

your——' She stumbled miserably, seeking a word which wouldn't be too evocative.

'Touch? Kisses? Lovemaking?' His amused voice prompted her. 'If that is so, then I can only say I must have been so carried away with my own pleasure that I was unaware of your distaste.'

'You . . .!' Verona stopped, unable to find a suitable noun to term him, too conscious of the implied truth behind his mild retort to condemn him as he deserved.

He gave a soft laugh at her discomfort, continuing easily, 'If it makes it any easier for you to accept my proposition, I'm quite prepared to promise I won't behave towards you in any way that would embarrass or upset Yana were she to be here to see us. Does that make you feel happier?'

Relief surged through her. There'd been nothing ambiguous about that statement!

'That would make me a lot happier,' she concurred, experiencing a pang of anxiety at the instant satisfaction that smoothed his personable face. The glint of triumph slid smoothly away as he continued his interrupted passage towards the door, pausing on the threshold.

'Then ι look forward to the coming days with much pleasure.'

CHAPTER EIGHT

THIRTEEN days later, Verona had to admit her fears had been groundless.

Leaning back on the sumptuously upholstered white leather cushions of the speedboat as it cut through the deep blue-black waters beneath the towering cliffs of the north coast, she sipped slowly from her wineglass.

Savouring the ice-cool flavour of the Minos Reservada, she allowed her gaze to rest indulgently on Andreas's back as he stood before her, steering the beautiful craft with a sure, loving touch.

She'd been astonished to find he owned such an expensive toy. Katina had never mentioned it, although the craft had been anchored out in the sheltered bay of Renagia.

Verona took another sip of the chilled wine, watching with a deep inner pleasure as Andreas turned the boat into the wind, and the combined effect of the speed and airflow caused his dark hair to ripple and his cool cotton shirt to billow away from his body, despite the mitigating presence of the high windscreen.

He stood, bare golden legs braced beneath brief hip-hugging shorts, staring out across the endless stretch of ocean. Verona couldn't see them, but she knew his eyes would be narrowed, his chin lifted as he enjoyed the pure physical pleasures of speed and freedom. He didn't need to stand. The boat was easily controllable from the driving seat. That he'd chosen to do so only served to confirm what she already knew about him. It gave him a more positive sensation of being fully in control. Poised and alert at the wheel, he became part of the beautiful, elegant craft, surging through the parting waters with total mastery of the environment.

Thirteen days—and Andreas had behaved with impeccable courtesy towards her. She smiled to herself, recalling how she'd started the time in trepidation, wondering how long she'd be able to exist in the company of her provocative host before hostility burgeoned between them. Yet from dinner on the first day through a series of events she'd been unable to fault him. The arrogant, supercilious, domineering Greek of her original encounter had been replaced by a gentler, considerate individual, no less masculine in attitude or beliefs but seemingly without the need to protect such an autocratic image. Watching his strong shoulders flex in pure enjoyment as the warm wind teased their flimsy covering, Verona mused over the preceding days, acknowledging the greater depths she had discovered in her imperious employer.

For a start, there was the religious streak he'd displayed while guiding her round Iraklion Cathedral. Unable to hide her astonishment, she'd watched him as, heavy-eyed, he'd lighted a candle to place before one of the holy statues.

Following his lead, she too had chosen a taper, sliding a ten-drachma piece into the box provided for payment, and placing it at the foot of the Virgin Mary with a silent prayer that Katina would find happiness in whatever destiny lay ahead of her.

When Andreas questioned her about her action she'd been hesitant.

'Surely if I tell you it won't come true?' she'd asked, with confused memories of childhood plaguing her, as she lifted clear hazel eyes in open doubt.

'That's wishes, *yatáki mou*,' he'd told her with a smile. 'Prayers gain in impact by being shared.'

So she'd confessed and been rewarded by a warm smile of approval. 'That's one prayer I can say "amen" to,' he'd responded instantly,

How she'd wished she'd dared to ask him what he'd prayed for. Somehow she couldn't, because if it concerned his future with Yana she didn't want to know. Unwilling to analyse her gut reaction to such a possibility, she'd changed the subject abruptly.

'I saw the notices on the walls,' she told him with genuine interest. 'Do men really have to sit on one side of the aisle and women on the other during a service?'

'But of course.' The startling blue eyes laughed at her. 'How can a Greek man sit beside a woman and keep his thoughts pure and holy as they should be in the sight of God?'

'Other men of different races manage it, I assume,' she'd mocked him, and his heritage. 'Are Greeks so totally without self-control?'

Andreas had shrugged nonchalant shoulders. 'Perhaps it's because we are more vital and virile than other men,' he'd offered, 'our responses more tuned and receptive to the temptations of the female than other races...more easily aroused and less easily satisfied, *né*?' He'd been so quietly confident of his sheer masculine prowess that the smile had died on her face as he continued to augment his argument. 'After all, the Greek Orthodox Church itself is prepared to acknowledge that forced celibacy is too great a burden to inflict on its acolytes, requiring only the highest members of its hierarchy to forgo the pleasure of love and marriage.'

Verona supposed she should have pointed out that the Protestant religion too adhered to St Paul's dictate that it was better to marry than burn, but at the time she hadn't wanted to discuss the matter further. Arguing about male virility with Andreas wasn't calculated to keep her blood cool. To be honest, she was becoming frighteningly aware that the initial attraction she'd felt for him hadn't diminished despite his unreasonable attitude in the past and his matrimonial plans for the future.

As time went on she was being forced to admit that Andreas pleasant was as disturbing to her as Andreas infuriating, and that her inadmissible love for him was flourishing with a disregard for Yana's claim that she found mortifying!

Stirring voluptuously where she sat, she lifted her face up towards the welcoming breeze and closed her eyes. The tour of Iraklion had been the first of many marvellous days. Impossible to rank in order of enjoyment, each one had held a sparkling magic of its own.

Would she ever forget the journey they'd taken up into the mountains, standing in splendid isolation with the scented herb-laden air a heady tang in their nostrils, gazing down into precipitous abysses between the soaring wind-carved rock-faces? She'd felt inexplicably dizzy, and when Andreas had put his strong arms round her shoulders, holding her tightly, pulling her against himself protectively, she'd been grateful, yet despairingly aware that her quickened heartbeat and trembling limbs weren't entirely due to the falling ground only yards ahead of her.

Every day they'd gone somewhere different. Andreas had shown off his island with pride and pleasure, telling her enough to make what she saw interesting, but never too much to bore her. Venetian castles, ancient Minoan ruins, museums, beaches, villages perched in the mountains, windswept plains with their bold array of windmills—the list was endless. Each new experience had burned its impression into her brain, subtly binding her to the homeland of her guide.

The day spent as guests of the Liviticos family had been especially illuminating. Katina had been radiant, flinging herself into Verona's arms the moment the two of them were alone in her bedroom.

'Oh, Verona! You can't imagine how I feel!' The younger girl's sparkling eyes were tear-bright with emotion. 'Stephanos is so wonderful—every day I wake up thinking I can never be happier—and every day, miraculously—I am!'

Six years between them, and Katina was suddenly fledged as a woman, secure in her own femininity and proud of her power to attract and entrance the young Greek who'd asked her brother's permission to court her. Gazing on her glowing, animated face, Verona found it impossible to suspect she was merely being an obedient sister to a strong-willed brother.

Katina was in love and it showed in every movement of her proud head, every flicker of her sweeping lashes and the sweet curve of her lovely mouth as she exchanged glances with Stephanos. That he was equally besotted, Verona didn't doubt any longer. More restrained and composed, he nevertheless made no attempt to hide the fact that his gaze was only torn away from Katina when the exigencies of polite conversation demanded it.

Now it was clear that Katina needed no shoulder on which to cry! Tentatively she had suggested to her friend that she might as well return to England once Katina's stay at Aghios Nicolaos was ended.

'But you can't!' A horror-stricken protest had greeted the suggestion. 'Hasn't Andreas been looking after you? He promised he'd do everything possible to make your stay happy or I would never have left you—even for Stephanos! And you did agree to stay until the end of the summer holiday! Oh, Verona, I'm sorry I left like that. But we can still enjoy ourselves together when I get back...' Her dark eyes filled with tears. 'I know I was selfish, but I really did believe Andreas would look after you. He knows the island so well and...'

'Your brother's spared no pains to give me an extended guided tour round Crete.' Verona had hastened to assure the Greek girl, knowing her tone was wooden but unable to infuse more emotion into it, so tightly contained were her muddled feelings towards Andreas Constanidou. Seeing the pained look on Katina's face, she added more graciously, 'I'm very grateful to him. He's even started to teach me how to speak Greek!'

'But you don't like him?' The younger girl's doleful face mirrored her disappointment.

Carefully Verona had avoided answering such a loaded question. What she felt for the handsome Greek was not something she was prepared to admit to herself, let alone acknowledge openly to his sister! She couldn't even comment on his relationship with Yana, since Andreas had assured her Katina knew nothing about his plans for marriage, and in her own interests he wanted it kept that way! Instead she'd sidestepped the problem. 'I feel I'm imposing on his time and hospitality.'

Katina had shaken her dark head firmly. 'No one imposes on Andreas. He doesn't allow it. If he's spending a lot of time with you it's because it pleases him to do so. Verona, please! Stephanos is leaving for Athens in a few days' time and I'm coming back to the villa. Please say you'll stay as long as you originally agreed.'

Verona frowned. She was neither needed nor wanted, and she should be getting back to England. The longer she left her search for a new job, the more difficult it would be. It was borne in on her painfully that she didn't want to leave. She didn't want to see an end to these halcyon days of sunshine and leisure. Shocked by her own weakness, she compromised.

'That depends on your brother.'

'Oh, that's all right, then!' Katina had been quietly confident. 'Andreas won't let you go.'

'Were you asleep?'

Verona's eyes opened with a start as she felt a gentle hand on her shoulder. Lost in contemplation of the past, she hadn't realised the boat had slowed dramatically.

'No—just daydreaming.' She returned Andreas's smile, combing her fingers through her windblown hair. 'Why have we stopped?'

He hadn't told her their destination, and she'd supposed they'd simply gone out for a sea trip.

She didn't receive an immediate answer as Andreas turned from her to cut the engine. The silence was deep and wonderful. To her left the cliffs rose sheer to a great height. On all other sides the ocean stretched a dark, cold blue, its movement a slow surge against the boat, making her stumble slightly as Andreas took her arm and drew her gently to her feet.

'See——' He pointed to the stark perpendicular rock devoid of vegetation. *'Kri-kri.'*

'Where?' Excitedly she shielded her eyes, straining to follow his pointing finger, searching for a sight of the legendary goat of Crete that lived on the high precipices.

'I can't...' she began, then drew in her breath with a hiss of astonishment. Not one, but two of them, balanced half-way down, seemingly on nothing. Her searching gaze saw no way to or from their precarious perch. It was as if they'd been plucked from the heavens and placed there by a divine hand. Above them the cliff towered smooth and perpendicular against the deep blue sky. Beneath them, by a hundred feet, it fell equally sheer into the even darker sea.

'No wonder they're nearly extinct,' she murmured. But the sight was awesome, and despite her attempt at levity Verona *was* impressed; the fact showed in her voice.

'Brave, foolhardy, taking their stand against a changing world, unable to compromise...' The hand that had guided her now tightened round her waist, as Andreas added meditatively, 'Perhaps there's a lesson for all of us there...look!'

As his voice sharpened on the last word his other hand rose to turn Verona's head forwards to where the cliff seemed to end in a ragged point. 'Watch! Do you see them?'

A sigh of satisfaction sang through the strong body of the man at her side as, still holding her firmly with one arm, Andreas shaded his own eyes with the other as the great bird to which he'd drawn Verona's attention glided towards them, wide wings spread, their serrated tips spread like dark fingers against the sky.

Even as she watched, entranced, it was joined by another in a graceful, perfect display of gliding. Moving across the sky on seven-foot wing-spreads, the two birds approached, soared overhead, circled and finally disappeared behind the cliffs.

'Eagles?' Excitement made Verona's voice tremble.

'White-tailed eagles.' Andreas nodded confirmation. 'They've been nesting here for the past two years, to my knowledge. It's unusual, because generally they're only found inland on the mountains.' He looked down at her. 'You're very privileged. Many times I've come here and not seen them. Yet, today, as soon as we arrive they come to greet you.'

'I've never seen anything like them before!' She smiled up into his face, her own countenance alive with joy. 'I'll never forget this day as long as I live, Andreas. They're so absolutely beautiful...'

'Not nearly as beautiful as you, Verona *mou*.'

His reaction took her by surprise. Hearing his voice laden with desire, she gasped, stepping backwards; forgetting how narrow the passage between the seats was, she overstepped, subsiding into the soft upholstery.

Andreas followed her down, his hands framing her face as his mouth sought her lips with hungry energy.

In that moment she forgot everything: Katina, Yana, the fact he considered her an inconsequential flirt. Only the present mattered. His sweet, warm breath, his strength, his demanding male body which conjured up a fierce answering response.

Dazed by the suddenness of his move, Verona parted her lips to receive and welcome his deep kiss, her arms enfolding him, her thighs moving to accommodate the hard male contours of his body as he pressed her down into the soft bench seat on which she rested. Then his fingers moved with predatory male directness to the heated curves of her aching breasts—and she came to her senses.

For thirteen days she had schooled herself to regard him as her friend's brother, her employer—even a friend. But never as a potential lover. He had helped her self-discipline by treating her with a respect she had cherished, and if her heart and body had ached for him, alone in her bed at night, then it had been a pain she'd known she must bear in silence, because there was no honourable alternative.

She'd lived in his house, shared his meals, experienced the pleasure of his company as he'd escorted her round Crete, filling her with his own love of the country that had bred him. She'd grown to trust him, come to believe that as his guest she'd be given the respect due to her. What a fool she'd been!

Realisation came as a cruel thrust of pain to her aroused body. It had been Andreas's purpose to seduce her from the moment he'd agreed to Katina's leaving the villa. With wicked cunning he'd lulled her fears, then carefully fed her a diet of excitement and discovery. Now, when the heady flow of adrenalin incited her body to an urgent response, he'd brought her to this isolated place, knowing she was too weak to fight him off if he persisted and that rescue was out of the question.

'No!' With a power born of desperation she pushed him away, her voice rising agonisingly as she realised the full seriousness of her predicament.

'No?' He seemed dazed, his voice husky and broken, his eyes glittering with brilliance as he stared into her taut face. 'You don't really mean that, do you, *yatáki mou*? You can't mean it!'

'Don't touch me!'

It was a hoarse plea, throbbing with emotion as Verona looked into Andreas's clear blue eyes, softened by the dilated darkness of impassioned pupils.

It had been madness, utter madness to allow him to kiss her. By responding so mindlessly she'd probably convinced him she was the wanton he'd already labelled her, fair game for any man—even one who'd already confirmed his intention of marrying another woman! Her blood ran cold at the thought. Heaven knew, she deserved his scorn. It wasn't as if she'd never heard of Yana Theodaxis or her role in his life, but in that instant of feeling Andreas's mouth against her own all other thoughts and considerations had vanished.

'What is it, *mahtia mou*? What's wrong, *agapi*?' Andreas's brows knitted in bewilderment as she stiffened beneath his predatory touch.

Panic-stricken, Verona felt her pulse race as her stomach knotted with tension. There was no place to run. She couldn't even escape from the purposeful caress of his lean hand as it touched her chin before sliding up to her hairline. Strong, sensual fingers laced through her silky tresses as Andreas made an inarticulate murmur deep in his throat.

'You know I want you,' he told her, his words low and disjointed. 'Since the moment I spoke to you at the airport and you turned to smile at me I've been obsessed by the thought of holding you, kissing you, making love to you. It's impossible that you didn't know!'

The boat was riding easily on the swell, lifting and sliding, taking Verona's body with it, forcing her into the dangerous caress of his arms as Andreas continued to stare down at her troubled countenance with a painful intensity.

'You've filled my dreams and haunted my waking hours; you've antagonised me and infuriated me, but above all you've made me desire you...'

'But I don't want *you*, Andreas!' she retorted desperately. 'I don't need a lover. I'm not one of your fast-living tourists, whatever you think!' She struggled to repel him, angry with him for breaking his word but twice as incensed with herself for being so trusting.

'Hush, *yatáki*...' He was humouring her. 'Do you think I haven't grown to know you better than that? But there's no need to pretend. You're not indifferent to me, *agapi*. You know we were meant for each other. Don't tease me, sweet Verona, admit it, tell me what I want to hear...or if you won't say it in words...show me!'

He crouched down at her feet his hands, resting either side of her suntanned thighs as he implored her. It was a position of humility, but there was nothing humble about Andreas Constanidou as his intense gaze searched the newly come pallor of her face.

'It's a lie!' Somehow she found the strength to oppose him, deeply aware of the potent threat he posed to her own self-respect. She couldn't, wouldn't be one of a number of women who passed through his life as surely as the seasons passed through the year. 'I don't want you, Andreas.' Sick and disillusioned by his approach and her own misjudgement for having encouraged it by agreeing to come on this lonely sea-trip with him, she fought down the welling fount of love that stirred in the depths of her body. His attitude had been impeccable these last days. She'd trusted him, and he'd deceived her.

'What kind of man are you, anyway?' she challenged fiercely. 'Isn't one woman at a time enough for you?'

'Definitely, as long as that woman is you.' He was blatantly unrepentant as he answered swiftly, his mouth curving into a smile that revealed the white perfection of his teeth. 'You can't deny the attraction between us. Yet, you ask me not to touch you? Sweet *yatáki*, you can't stop an avalanche with words!'

He rose to draw her into his embrace, but she fought with her last ounce of strength, angered by the way he was using her, as if she were an easy pick-up instead of his sister's friend and companion. How dared he plan her seduction with such gracious diligence? And, worst of all—how dared she feel the way she did at this moment—yielding and warm and wanton? Wasn't it bad enough that she had to fight this arrogant specimen of Hellenic manhood, without the need to fight her own desires?

Her growing temper lent her an added strength as she finally jerked away from his reaching arms. 'If you're so desperate for a woman, why don't you go back to Yana?' she snarled. 'She's obviously not as choosy as I am!'

Instantly the words had left her tongue she regretted them. Andreas had named her 'kitten', but that last remark had been worthy of a cat. A nervous pulse in her throat betrayed her agitation as she waited apprehensively for his reaction.

'Yana!' he muttered. '*Theo mou*, I'd forgotten about Yana...' His dark head tilted to one side as eyes bright beneath narrowed lids surveyed her thoughtfully. 'Jealous, Verona? There's no need to be. Yana means nothing to me.'

'The woman you intend to marry means nothing?' She stared at him in horror, edging along the seat as he settled down easily beside her, his body blocking any hope of escape—even if there'd been any sanctuary for her except the deep dark waters that swelled beneath them. 'That's the cruellest, most unfeeling thing I've ever heard you say!'

'You're right.' The words were calm enough, but there was a glint in his eyes that made the short hairs on her neck bristle. 'Of course Yana means something to me.' He paused. 'She's one of the best, most talented fabric designers I've had the fortune to employ.'

His cruel dismissal of the woman was horrifyingly cold-blooded. More than Verona could tolerate.

'Is sharing your bed one of the conditions of employment?' she demanded scathingly. 'Or was Yana particularly chosen because of her skills? A Greek girl with a traditional Greek's philosophy, and a talented one to wit! No wonder you found her irresistible. While you're out womanising she'll be at home sweating over a hot drawing-board!' Her voice seethed with a militant fury as she threw caution to the winds. 'I don't know the kind of women you're used to going out with. Perhaps some of them wouldn't care about your commitment to Yana, but not me, Andreas! *I* care very much!'

She was shaking, so incensed that she'd forgotten the danger she was courting until Andreas seized her with ungentle hands. 'You talk too much, *yatáki*!' Her unwilling mouth was possessed with a deadly purpose as she struggled to evade him.

As he pinned her to the seat with his weight, Verona felt his hands seek out her body, moving languidly over its curves, touching her breasts through the light cotton covering of her T-shirt. She shivered as they lingered with delicate purpose on the hardening apexes that responded automatically to their caress.

Humiliated because she was unable to hide the way he was able to arouse her, Verona felt tears stinging her eyes. Then the insolent kiss changed its tenor, gentled, became persuasive. She mustn't allow herself to be seduced by his practised tenderness! Andreas was unfaithful and arrogant. Everything she detested in a man. How could she ache with such painful longing beneath the caress of his tongue and hands?

His lips brushed hers slowly before withdrawing. It could have been worse, she supposed, raising her slim fingers to touch their bruised tissue. He could have struck her for daring to taunt him about his morals. On second thoughts, perhaps a blow wouldn't have been worse. It might have left her more physically damaged, but it wouldn't have hurt her in the same way as that brutal, strangely compelling kiss.

His face was still only inches from her own. She could see the moisture clinging to his top lip, the dark dampness of the mouth that had plundered her so ruthlessly. Inside she was weak and defeated, unable to stop the tears spilling on to her cheeks.

'Forgive me, Verona....' His voice was laboured, his breathing heavy as he lifted one forefinger to touch the moisture on her face. 'I've let you believe a lie for a long time—too long. The truth is, Yana has never been other than an employee to me. Valued and respected, but nothing more.'

'But...?' Bewildered, she asked silently for an explanation, hardly daring to believe what her ears had told her.

'You deserve an explanation,' he said sombrely, 'and I can only hope you'll understand when you hear it. You see, Yana fell in love with Grafton a couple of years ago. Despite her family's stern opposition she moved in with him, believing eventually he would marry her.' He shrugged broad shoulders. 'Yana is, as you say, a Greek girl and her roots demand marriage from the man she takes as a lover. But as time went on it was clear Grafton was content to live with her without making it legal. In the end she couldn't accept it. She decided to cut free from him once and for all.'

'And she asked for your help?' Intrigued, Verona stifled the small sobs that Andreas's retribution had invoked.

'Not directly.' He grimaced as if the memory was painful. 'But we had a big order on hand and Yana was working well below standard. I called her in and demanded to know what was the matter. She confessed everything, including the fact that her parents had disowned her the day she moved in with Grafton. It appeared she'd moved in with a friend after making the break, but this girl was expecting a baby and needed the extra room. Yana had been trying to find accommodation but without success, and the worry was making her ill. I had to take action for all our sakes.'

CHAPTER NINE

THERE was a moment's silence before Verona said slowly, 'So you offered to let her stay in your apartment in Iraklion?' Light dawned as she watched his head dip in assent.

'As a temporary solution while I was away in Athens. When I returned I sent her to a friend of mine who runs a small hotel. He let her have good accommodation at a very reasonable rate as a favour to me, and I promised I wouldn't let Grafton know where she was.'

'And that's where she is now?' For so long she'd believed Andreas had a mistress, she could hardly believe what she was hearing.

'Actually, no.' He tossed her a wry smile. 'At this moment she's back living with Grafton—preparing designs for her wedding-dress.'

'She's what?' Her own bitterness forgotten, Verona responded with astonishment to his assertion.

'A happy outcome for which you must take the credit.' He nodded affirmatively.

'Me?' Stunned hazel eyes looked at him dazedly.

'Certainly.' Blue eyes danced with amusement at her astonishment. 'I was in no mood to act as go-between on Grafton's behalf, but I had to get him away from you. Every time I saw the two of you together I was eaten up with jealousy.' He made a deprecating motion with one hand. 'Besides ... Yana was still in love with him, despite all her protestations to the contrary! What she really wanted was marriage, not separation, but she

156

wasn't going to settle for less, and she'd lost all hope of Grafton's ever proposing.'

'But—you'd promised to keep her address a secret?'

'Yes.' Andreas nodded. 'But after you left us at the taverna, Grafton told me he wouldn't stop trying to find her, even if it meant breaking up our wedding service, and I decided things had gone far enough.'

'She *had* told Bob, then, that she was going to marry you?' She'd been wondering if Bob had lied about that for some devious purpose of his own.

For a moment Andreas's eyes gleamed with humour. 'Yes, I'm afraid she did. It was her way of telling him that unless he wanted her enough to offer her similar terms she would never go back to him. So,' he lifted a faintly cynical eyebrow, 'I decided the best thing to do was to let Grafton tell her just what he *did* propose. I told him if he had anything constructive to say to her he should write it down and I'd see she got it.' Blue eyes, thickly lashed, sparkled at her. 'It seemed he made a very good job of his letter—but then, what would one expect? He is a scriptwriter, after all!'

'But...' Verona's head was spinning. 'But *you* let me think you were going to marry her...' She looked at him accusingly. 'I told you I thought that was what you meant to do—why?'

'I didn't confirm it, just let you go on believing what you did,' he interrupted her briskly, then uttered a long-drawn-out sigh. 'You were determined to think the worst of me, weren't you, *yatáki mou*? You had me stereotyped as a callous brute who'd marry off his teenage sister to further his own interests, and you hated yourself for being attracted to me...'

'Andreas!' she protested, colour flooding into her face, but he refused to listen to her, waving aside her attempted interruption with a peremptory flick of his hand.

'I wanted to be with you, share my home and my country with you. I wanted us to get to know each other better... but it seemed impossible until Stephanos invited Katina to stay with his parents. I'd made a bad impression with you from the start, due to my own prejudices and impatience, and I needed to let you see what I was really like. But I knew you would never have agreed to stay in the villa with me alone unless you imagined my affections were engaged elsewhere, would you? You would have packed your case and left without giving me the chance to show you how good we would be together. So,' a dismissive wave of his hands, 'when Bob relayed what Yana had told him I played along with it.'

How well he'd read her apprehension! A shiver trickled down her spine.

'You were wrong to make me stay.' She turned sombre eyes to his smiling face. 'I'm not interested in casual affairs. I never have been.'

'Neither am I.'

The prompt reply brought a cynical turn to her lips. She might accept that his association with Yana had been platonic, but Andreas Constanidou was no celibate. She'd stake her life on it.

'Truly...' He was all injured innocence. 'My days of philandering are in the past. I admit that for a time, after my first initiation into the art of love undertaken by a "friend" of Papa's when I was sixteen, I wasn't particularly choosy. But when my father died I found trying to keep the business stable used up most of my available energy... and time. Since then...' He gave a casual shrug of his broad shoulders. 'Since then, *yatáki mou*, I've become very, very selective.' Once more his hands lifted towards her. 'I don't deny I've had many women friends, but for the most part that's what they remained—just friends!'

'So am I selective.' Verona made a grab for his wrists before his hands achieved their purpose. 'And I don't select you, Andreas!' Her head came up proudly as her green-flecked gaze defied him. 'When I make love with a man it's because I'm in love with him, not just to satisfy a physical impulse.' Yet it was the physical impulse that was racking her body at that moment, shortening her breath and bringing a tingle to her breasts. She forced herself to be firm. 'Now, can we please go back to Renagia?'

His hands lay quiescent in hers as Andreas met her hostile stare. Please God he didn't guess the inward battle she was fighting, and how much it was costing her. But, even without the complication of Yana, very little had changed. To love and to leave had never been a part of her philosophy. For years she had made her head rule her heart. Now was not the time to change the habit of a lifetime.

'Would it make a difference if I told you I loved you?' he asked softly, striking at the soft underbelly of her resistance with a fiendish cruelty.

'No!' She rejected the suggestion with the contempt it deserved. 'Don't treat me like a fool, Andreas. Do you think I don't know those are the first words every Mediterranean man learns in English because he knows they're what the gullible female tourist wants to hear— the magic phrase that quietens her conscience, persuades her she's not promiscuous when she tears off her clothes to satisfy the greedy, unfeeling man who preys on her?' Choking on her hurt, she turned her face away from him. 'I told you. I'm not like that! Please take me back.'

'So you despise me,' he returned harshly. 'God knows, I can't blame you. I've certainly given you enough reason to hate me, but try to understand. These past weeks you've turned my life upside-down. I sensed there could be something special between us the moment I set eyes on you!' He gave an exasperated sigh, while she sat motionless, trying to control the rapid pounding of her heartbeat. 'Then, when I discovered who you were, I was furious because the circumstances put you beyond my reach. How could I get involved with the woman who was to be my sister's chaperon? And yes, I admit it, I was afraid your liberated views on life could prejudice Katina's long-term happiness.'

'Liberated . . .' she breathed the word. 'You misjudged me badly at the time,' she told him with quiet dignity. 'And you're still doing it.'

'Try to understand a little and forgive me.' He made no attempt to touch her, but his eyes demanded her attention. 'I had very little reason to think kindly of you at the beginning. Listen, Verona, I'm going to tell you something very few people know—not even Kati.' He leaned back against the soft upholstery as he continued harshly, 'My parents' marriage wasn't a happy one...and before you ask me, no, it wasn't an arranged one. I imagine my mother would have been far happier if it had been.'

'Go on,' Verona encouraged him quietly as he paused, aware of the privilege she was being granted by this insight into his background.

'My father came from Northern Greece to carry out business here in Crete. He saw my mother and fell in love with her on the spot. Not only was she beautiful but virtuous too, so because he wanted her he married her and took her back to the mainland with him.' He paused, staring sightlessly ahead. 'It was a disaster. Mama was an island girl, educated at home to be a competent wife in the environment she knew. She was desperately homesick away from Crete, pregnant and miserable, so my father brought her back, but it was no good. She wasn't his intellectual equal and, worse still, she didn't want to be. She couldn't understand what he wanted from her, let alone give it to him. So,' he shrugged his shoulders, 'he went out and found his pleasure elsewhere. Tourism was under way, and he found its by-products offered him an escape from the prison he'd made for himself. After I was born, he didn't even share her bed.'

'But Katina...?' Verona halted, confused.

'Was the product of a moment's desperation, he once told me.'

'I'm sorry.' Verona placed a sympathetic hand on Andreas's arm. 'You must have had an unhappy childhood.'

'No,' he denied. 'Both my parents loved me, and when Katina was born there seemed to be some hope for them, but it didn't last.' He took Verona's hand between his two palms. 'I told you my father was drowned. Well, at the time he was out on a hired boat with an English tourist—a married woman who was on holiday with her husband and young son. Their only relationship was physical.' His voice deepened with pain. 'When the accident occurred she was terrified, not for my father's life but for her own reputation and the survival of her marriage. It was hours before she plucked up courage to inform the coastguard—and by then it was too late.'

'Oh, Andreas, how awful!' For the first time she caught a glimpse of the underlying cause of his early antagonism. To desire her had been a weakness, and one that could have threatened Katina's happiness for the second time...

'It was—grim,' he accorded sternly. 'Of course it was inevitable that my mother found out the truth. I believe she could have borne his death with a greater fortitude if she hadn't discovered exactly how it had come about. Naturally she'd had her suspicions, but while he was discreet she'd closed her mind to his wandering. For him to die in such circumstances was not only tragic but humiliating—not just for her, but him too.'

'That's dreadful...' Verona tried to imagine the shock and distress of Andreas's mother. The shame she would have felt.

Andreas made a dismissive movement with his shoulders, continuing to speak in a bleak monotone. 'After my father's death I made two resolutions. One was that my sister should never suffer the fate of my mother. She would be educated and sophisticated and become the wife of a man who would appreciate her for what she was. And the second was, I swore never to get deeply involved with the women who came here for the summer and returned to their homes to boast to their friends about the "bit of Greek" they enjoyed, as if a man's possession of them was worth no more to them than a glass of *ouzo* or a helping of *moussaka*...'

Shocked by the bitterness of the words, Verona's puzzled glance dwelt on the harsh lines of Andreas's face, forced to re-examine her own beliefs. It had never occurred to her that a man could consider himself used by a woman, and the realisation stunned her. But Andreas was continuing, speaking softly but firmly. 'So when I first found myself aching for you like some crass teenager, I was disgusted at what you were able to do to me. But I couldn't fight it. And as I observed the way you were with Kati I realised you were different from the flighty blondes who parade themselves for male approval with no thought for consequences. I knew then that we were meant to be lovers.'

Ignoring her soft moan of protest, he repeated huskily, 'Lovers, *yatáki mou*. But I'd hurt you and I knew I had to win your forgiveness before you'd come to me, so when Katina was invited to Aghios Nicolaos I saw it as the opportunity I needed to repair all the harm I'd done.'

'You succeeded very well, Andreas.' Her flat tone both condemned and praised his cunning. Perhaps she should be flattered by the careful road he'd taken to seduction. Instead, all she felt was a heavy depression. 'Over these last few days I've grown to like you very much.' It was the least and the most she could tell him. 'Does that satisfy you?'

'Like—is that all?' His mouth twisted wryly. 'No, it doesn't satisfy me, but for the moment it will have to do.'

This time she couldn't prevent the power of his strong arms from their purposeful embrace. When his mouth brushed her forehead, travelled down her cheek and sought her lips, she knew it would be futile to resist him.

He was murmuring words of Greek to her, his voice a soft growl as he held her beneath him on the soft bench. Wild thoughts rushed through her brain. He could take her now with only the empty sky and sea as witnesses to her mindless surrender. For all her reason, she couldn't find the energy to restrain him. Her arms enfolded him, enjoyed the hard maturity of his powerful back and shoulders. Dear heavens . . . but he was beautiful and she loved him . . . despite everything!

She found herself suddenly released as Andreas backed away, rose to his feet, standing looking down at her flushed face. A slow tide of pleasure flowed through her veins as she became shockingly aware of the response within her own body. Petrified, she watched Andreas's tall figure as slowly he lifted his shirt over his head, revealing his bronzed, gleaming torso. Her breath caught in her throat as a great wave of longing invaded every cell beneath her warm flesh. He swayed slightly with the motion of the boat and his eyes, darkened with desire, never left her face.

'Take off your top.' His words were heavy, barely audible. 'Please, my darling, I want to look at you.'

The words roused a chord of memory as they pierced through her languor. Andreas half-naked as he was now, his impertinent scrutiny roaming her tense form as she'd faced him on the beach. What had he said? 'When the time comes for me to enjoy the sight of your unclad body it will give me the greatest pleasure to know it's a privilege not already extended to the community in general and my fellow countrymen in particular . . .'

He hadn't cared for her then—and he didn't care for her now! His blithe protestations were slick and unbelievable. At the best she was no more than a summer's diversion to him, baited like a fish on a hook from the moment her hazel eyes had recoiled from his ice-blue appraisal. At the worst she was being punished for the sins of an unknown Englishwoman whose immorality and cowardice had robbed him of a father!

Yet her body trembled with the need to obey him, to strip off her top and allow his avid gaze to devour her naked breasts. Her swollen nipples had responded to his husky command by thrusting themselves in hard contention against the soft fabric of their covering.

Mutual desire burned like a flame between them, but she had to deny it. To have sex without love was anathema to her, and he didn't love her. He might find her desirable, even like her, but it wasn't enough. Her hands rose protectively to shield her aroused body from his gaze in case he read its message too clearly, and she had to clench her teeth in an effort to control her trembling lips.

'No, Andreas.' She gulped, aware of his steady contemplation. 'You've misunderstood how I feel. This isn't what I want...you have to believe me!' She searched his handsome face for any sign of amnesty. Surely he wouldn't sink to taking her by force?

'What *do* you want, Verona? Are you sure you know?' There was a sadness in his deep voice that touched her as much as his previous passion, but she was resolute.

'To return to Renagia!' Her voice rose emphatically as she insisted in denying him.

There was a tiny pause while she held her breath. When Andreas moved suddenly, making for the bow of the boat to switch the dashboard key, and she heard the engine burst into life, she knew she'd won. Only, there was no joy in the victory. Just a sense of loss and desolation, and a hungry emptiness that spread its icy fingers through every fibre of her weary body.

Two o'clock in the morning and not a breath of wind. Verona hoisted herself up in bed. Heavens—but it was hot! The *meltimi*, Andreas had told her as he'd helped her to jump on to the small jetty where he moored the boat, blowing straight from the Sahara carrying the desert sand in its scorching breath, baking the ground and enervating the population. In these conditions the temperature could rise into the high nineties Fahrenheit, dropping by only a few degrees at night.

She swung her legs out of bed. Clammy and uncomfortable, her hair lying damp against her neck, her short nightdress sticking to her body, she longed for a cold shower. Perhaps if she was quiet she could steal one without waking Andreas in the adjoining room?

Silently she padded to the bathroom, stripping off the clinging nylon and turning on the shower, allowing the cool cascade of water to stream refreshingly over her burning skin.

Beneath its cool caress she mused on the events of the day. How easy it would have been to succumb to Andreas's practised caresses, to yield to their mutual pleasure in the open air with the depth of the sea beneath them and the vault of heaven above. How pagan and wonderful...and disastrous! It was going to be hard enough to rout his memory from her mind as it was. Yet it was something she would have to do once she resumed her old life.

Sighing, she blotted herself dry, towelling the moisture from her hair before returning to the bedroom to find another nightdress.

Once they'd entered the villa, Andreas's attitude had been cool and formal, a welcome relief from what she'd feared. It seemed he'd taken 'no' as a final answer; but she'd been uneasy, jumpy in his presence, turning down his invitation for dinner at one of the tavernas, saying she preferred to have a snack indoors, then rest.

Rest! That was a laugh. She slipped the deep rose chiffon nightdress over her head, appreciating the soft, silken feel as it tantalised her newly cooled skin. She'd done precious little resting.

Gazing down at the crumpled bed, she knew sleep would continue to elude her. Perhaps outside on the terrace she could find a trace of a breeze. Warm though it would undoubtedly be, it would be preferable to the still heat that encompassed her inside the villa.

Stealthily she made her way outside, feeling a soft curl of wind tease her hair as soon as her bare feet touched the warm stones. Warm and scented, it breathed against her skin. Thankfully she inhaled it, savouring its perfume tinged with the aroma of wild herbs from two continents. Turning towards its source, she walked to the far end of the terrace where the latter cornered the building—and came to an abrupt halt.

Andreas lay at her feet. Naked except for a brief pair of cotton shorts, he was spreadeagled on an inflatable air bed, on his back, head turned to one side, arms limp, one knee raised and slightly slewed. For all the world like a warrior slain in battle, she determined, a warm affection filtering through her, followed instantly by a painful constriction of her throat as she cursed a fate cruel enough to bring her here, allowing her to drink her fill of him, when all she wanted to do was rip the last thread of memory of him from her brain.

Thick lashes fanned his hard cheeks; his mouth was a tender curve with slightly parted lips. Verona's teeth clamped on her own lower lip. She must turn and go before her hard-won resolve melted in the deep warmth of the Cretan night. Still her gaze lingered, leaving the dark thickness of his hair to trail an unmarked path from his chest downwards past his neat navel, skimming the cloth-covered loins, enjoying the hard, full beauty of his long, supple legs. He was incredibly desirable—and she would have been less of a woman if she didn't recognise that fact with every fibre of her being—and less of a rational human being if she couldn't control the weakness of her own flesh, she lectured herself sternly!

She must go—now, before the wild beating of her heart made movement impossible and he awakened hours later to find her immobile as a statue, still poised admiringly above him! She allowed herself a small smile as her eyes fluttered in one last self-indulgence over his sleeping face, her mouth opening in a small cry as she observed a mosquito poised threateningly over one dark eyebrow.

Without a second thought she was on her knees at Andreas's side, her fingers flicking towards the intruder, brushing it away before it could inject its poison.

'It is you, *yatáki mou* . . . not a dream . . .'

As an arm curled round her, preventing her from rising to her feet, Verona gasped in shocked dismay.

'I came out for a breath of air,' she explained her presence breathlessly. 'You were going to get bitten . . .'

'Then go ahead and bite me, *agapi*. But be warned . . . I may bite back!'

In the starlight she saw the smile that twisted his lips and grooved his cheeks as Andreas pulled himself up lazily into a sitting position, still restraining her with one arm. 'But shall we start slowly . . . like this, perhaps?'

Not waiting for a reply, he caught Verona to him, teasing her mouth with his kiss, sweetly and gently, applying a romantic caress that brought the blood thrumming to her ears. When he released her lips she couldn't speak as a deep impulse of tenderness conjured an aching lump to her throat.

'Is that the way you like to be loved, sweet *yatáki*?' he demanded softly.

This was her chance to say she didn't welcome any caress from him, but it was too late. It would be a lie and he would know it. Her thoughts in a turmoil, Verona hung her head.

'No answer, hmm?' His hands, so firm and capable, drifted downwards, found the hem of her nightdress and, ignoring her soft gasp of shock, slid beneath it to rest softly against her bare waist. 'Don't lie to me again, *mahtia mou*. Don't pretend with me. This afternoon on the boat you wanted me as much as I longed for you. Haven't you made me suffer enough? Am I still to be punished for the mistakes I've made?'

Before the soft intensity of the question and the piercing impact of his eyes, Verona quailed. How could she answer such questions? But the touch of his hand against her skin was like an electric shock, painful and stimulating, forcing the truth from her unwilling lips.

'It's not a punishment, Andreas...' she managed huskily. 'I don't want to hurt you...'

'No?' The word was a slow sigh of hope. 'Then stop torturing me, my sweet. Can't you see we were made for each other like yogurt and honey?'

'An acquired taste...' She forced her mouth to smile as she tried to be light-hearted, the dull lethargy of her limbs preventing the movement she knew she should make away from his devastating presence.

'To which I'm addicted...'

As he pulled her to him it was as if something inside her finally snapped, as if the rigid self-control stretched too tightly had given under the strain. In that moment all fight vanished from her, her lips opening like a flower before the onslaught of the sun, accepting him, inviting him, taking the initiative, drawing him into herself in an abandonment of longing.

There was no particular reason for her sudden surrender. It happened involuntarily, this unexpected moment of her total capitulation, and they both recognised it for what it was.

Crushing her warm, pliant body to his own nakedness, Andreas pulled her back on to the soft bed, turning with her, pressing her into the resilient air cushion. Triumphantly aware she was offering no resistance, he kissed her with a heady power that made her senses reel. Overwhelmed by his touch, taste and scent, Verona could only cling to him as the final breach of her defences left her totally vulnerable to his ardent caresses.

When his hands carefully slipped the fine fabric of her nightdress over her head to discard it completely, she stretched her body, displaying herself shamelessly for his pleasure, her heart beating a wild tattoo of exultation as his face darkened with a strange intense passion and he gazed his fill on the pale flesh the sun had never seen.

'I have dreamed of this moment…' His voice was thick with passion as he traced the pale curves with a hand that trembled. 'Just for me…*mahtia mou*…for my eyes alone.' Almost reverently he stroked his fingers against the pulsating curves of her breasts, increasing the gentle pressure to a stronger, more insistent massage as her breath quickened, his thumbs inciting her erect nipples to an aching peak of response, before lowering his mouth to their swollen tips in a gentle act of homage.

Quivering with a fierce, painful pleasure, Verona tightened her grasp on his shoulders. His mouth was a delicate, taunting visitor, making her writhe, turning her body into one great void of longing from which there was no way back. Not that she was considering retreat, as Andreas followed the length of her form with the sensitive fingers of one hand, tracing a path from hip to thigh, moving inexorably to the heart of her need for him. He had been right. This moment had been written in her stars...

Every nerve and muscle awakened to him; every organ in her body seemed to exist only for his joy; every pore of her skin exuded the evidence of her desire, unconsciously taunting the man who pleasured her with the musky perfume of its source, as Verona instinctively returned his gestures of love. Relaxing to his touch, she reached to stroke and smooth the warm, enticing skin of his fine male body, hearing him moan, a deep, animal sound, as her gentle hand caressed him.

'Did—did I hurt you?' she faltered, shocked by the agony of the response her exploring fingers had brought forth. For the first time in her life she wished she'd been more experienced. Oh, she was one hundred per cent OK with the theory, she thought a trifle hysterically, remembering the warm, understanding discussions she'd had with her mother during her puberty, not to mention the more clinical analyses of her later years at school, but nothing had prepared her for the reality.

'Do you want me, *yatáki mou*?' It was such a quiet whisper, the question that was about to change her life. And it *was* a question, not a statement. He hadn't told her she wanted him...Andreas had asked her...and even though he must have known the answer, she appreciated it.

Shaking, weak and receptive to his total possession, she was desperate to yield, to seek a sweet armistice beneath the turbulent force of her lover's body. Andreas might not love her, but he was a man of compassion. She thought fleetingly of the people he had loved—his parents, his sister—his pity for Yana when she needed help, and her need to return to him in some measure the powerful emotion he had expended on others was an

uncontrollable urge. She wanted him, yes. She wanted
Andreas to love her but, more than that, she wanted to
love him. Needed to love him in the fullest, surest way
possible. Instinctively she knew that her love was strong
enough to justify for both of them the events that must
surely come to pass within the following minutes.

'Oh, yes, Andreas *mou*!' she told him joyfully. 'Oh,
yes . . . yes . . . yes!'

CHAPTER TEN

SHE was flying. At one with the night and the stars, naked in the night air, mortal yet somehow immortal as well. For the long, lingering moments while Andreas worshipped her body to bring her to the level of his own receptiveness, it was as if she was living on another plane, but when the moment came for him to pierce the delicate tissue deep within her, it was Andreas's name she cried aloud, Andreas's shoulders she bit into as he arched and thrust above her. Heart thundering, breath sawing, she was teetering on the brink of oblivion, and when he took her to it and beyond it, it was Andreas's lips which licked the salt tears of joy from her cheeks, Andreas's kisses which eventually stilled her low moans of passion fulfilled.

For several minutes they lay without speaking as Verona listened to the heavy rhythm of Andreas's breathing. For the first time in her life she felt truly alive, she realised with quiet wonder, as if an extra dimension had been added to her existence. And she now knew, with a devastating clarity, that all her earlier scruples had been justified. She'd been right to wait for someone she really loved. That was the biggest truth of all.

Beside her Andreas stirred, his relaxed body still splendidly male with its coiled muscles and powerful sinews.

'Katina will be overjoyed when she knows about us.'

'Katina?' Verona returned to reality with a bump. 'You're going to tell your sister that we . . . that you and

I . . .' She faltered miserably. She hadn't even considered the future but, if she was going to stay, it was only natural that Andreas would expect them to be lovers. It was something she should have thought about before, she realised miserably. To her, what had just happened between them had been the culmination of her love for Andreas; to him, it had been the beginning of a brief but continuing affair. But it was impossible. Surely he wouldn't expect to banish Kati to the single room and share the double with her? Even if he decided to take her to his Iraklion flat, it would be a dreadful betrayal of her friendship with his sister . . .

'That we are going to be married?' Andreas finished her sentence, amusement and a sureness of purpose lending depths to his pleasant voice. 'But of course I am. She'll be delighted to have you as a sister-in-law.'

'Married?' Verona's voice rose half a tone. 'Did you say married, Andreas?' For no apparent reason she felt sick, a prey to a hundred and one doubts and fears. 'But—but that's impossible!' Her hazel eyes widened in anxiety as she took in the sombre lines of his face. 'Why should we be married? You—you don't love me, Andreas!'

This was the moment he should quash her doubts, tell her he *did* love her, that, like her, he couldn't have made love to her unless his heart had been involved. Only he didn't. Hadn't he already admitted to her that in his early youth at least he had had no difficulty in satisfying his male appetite without the need for caring? Why should time alone have changed him?

'You're hardly flattering, *yatáki mou*.' He looked at her quizzically. 'I thought I had just proved my love for you in a most satisfactory way, *né*?'

'That's not enough reason for marriage.' Dry-throated, she reached to collect her abandoned nightdress, slipping it over her head, covering her satiated body from his steady stare, aware of the frown that puckered his broad forehead and the note of contention in his deep voice. 'My life is in England. I haven't even begun on the kind of career I want. Besides, you should marry a Greek girl, someone like Yana...' She was babbling on, confused by his attitude, unable to understand what had prompted him to make such a bizarre proposal.

'Nevertheless,' he told her smoothly, 'I was your first lover and I intend to be your last!' Adamant and positive, the old Andreas had replaced the ardent lover with his accustomed autocratic self.

Verona felt her skin tingle with anticipation, as a wave of apprehension made her blood run cold. So that was it! Now she knew the reason for her previously unaccountable qualms. She should have told him she'd never had a lover rather than let him discover the fact for himself, but at the time it had never crossed her mind to do so. If anything, she'd assumed he would remain unaware of her virginity—but she'd been wrong. Now he obviously felt that it was his ethical duty to make an 'honest' woman of her! Dear God, as if she would ever agree to a marriage based on Andreas's disgust with himself for violating what he saw as his responsibility towards his sister's friend!

'I'm sorry, Andreas...' She made a helpless gesture with both hands. 'I suppose I should have warned you, but you must realise you're under no obligation to me.' His frown deepened, causing her to rush on before he could interrupt. 'You know I haven't been brought up as strictly as girls here in Greece are. Back home, many girls experiment...'

'Experiment! You dare to tell me what happened between us was an experiment!' His fury shimmered, controlled only by a massive will-power as Verona shrank back from his voluble anger.

'No, of course not,' she hastened to calm him, surprisingly near to tears and unable in her distress to find the right words to explain that she, unlike Yana, expected nothing further from him.

'Then there's no further argument.' Stubbornness stiffened his jaw. 'Once the necessary formalities have been taken care of, you will become my wife.'

'No!' Verona surprised herself by the vehemence of her reply. 'Oh, can't you see, Andreas, marriage between us would never work, not on the basis of what has just happened? Remember how unhappy your own parents were because all they had was physical attraction instead of love . . .' She licked her parched lips, searching in her mind for other areas that would disunite them, but before she could gather her wits together her task was aborted by Andreas's harsh interruption.

'They were intellectually incompatible—that's what stifled them.' He subjected her to a raking scrutiny. 'Is that what worries you? You would find marriage to me too small a challenge, *yatáki*?' he queried fiercely. 'It wouldn't stretch your capabilities enough...to share my life...bear my child? Oh, Verona...' He shook his dark head. 'Do you really think you can find a bigger challenge in life than the one I can offer you?' He paused to touch her soft mouth with a remonstrative finger. 'For a start, my ignorant beauty, you shall learn Greek properly—you already show a talent for it. If the poorest uneducated peasant in Crete can speak it, then so can you! Then, when you are fluent, you shall have a position in my company dealing with people—not computers.' A smile lightened his eyes. 'Perhaps if it had been to you Yana Theodaxis had turned in her hour of need, her troubles would have been solved much sooner, eh?' He laughed down into her troubled eyes.

'Andreas...please...'

'Still not enough scope for you?' Once more he brushed aside her attempt to interrupt him. 'Soon I shall be setting up an office in Los Angeles. Would travelling to the States stretch you sufficiently, I wonder?'

'Stop it, please, Andreas!' She was near to breaking point. She didn't want to hear any more. She didn't want to think about bearing his children or travelling to the States. She didn't want to be influenced by his hard-applied bribes or bought by an assortment of goodies. She'd given in to the power of her own sexuality and she wasn't ashamed of it, nor did she regret it. How could she, when every fibre of her being still gloried in the intimate knowledge of Andreas Constanidou? But marriage was too high a price to pay for that lingering moment of tumultuous joy she had experienced, when Andreas's offer was based on preserving his own pride...rather than on loving her!

She shuddered, imagining what it would be like loving him and being forced to watch him seeking relationships outside a union that wasn't of his original choosing. Impossible to expect her to accept such a situation with the equanimity Katina had accorded to her Greek counterparts!

'It's too late now to ask me to stop!' Andreas argued swiftly, a hard muscle jerking spasmodically in his jaw as she recoiled spontaneously from his harsh anger. 'You should have thought about what you were doing before you made yourself vulnerable to bearing my child!'

'So that's what's worrying you!' Glaring at his stubbornly set face as he confirmed and intensified her worst fears, Verona felt an urgent desire to slap him. Not that it would do her any good. In his present truculent mood Andreas would probably repay the insult with interest. At the same time a lance of disquiet pierced her complacency. She had never intended things to go so far so fast, and had been totally unprepared both mentally and physically for the celebration of desire they had both enjoyed.

Presumably Andreas, convinced of her promiscuity on no evidence other than his own prejudices, had been labouring under the misapprehension that she was prepared for chance encounters. The thought brought the hot blood rushing to her face. Only minutes ago she had been bathed in euphoria. Now she'd been brought down to earth with a shock. A quick calculation afforded her a measure of relief.

'Relax, Andreas. It's a very remote possibility,' she informed him coldly. 'The odds against it are so great, it doesn't merit your sacrificing your bachelorhood and marrying one of your despised "tourists". And be assured it's the last thing I want or need from you, although I appreciate the courtesy of your gesture.'

'So you're like all the others, after all.' Bitterness echoed in his response. 'I'd really begun to believe you were different.' His dark brows rose in derision. 'Tell me, Verona, why me? Why did you choose me to be the first?'

She caught her breath, hating the cruel slant of his cynical smile. No way would she tell him the truth, confess that she loved him, when all his interest was self-centred. She shrugged her shoulders, lifting her head to meet his cold eyes with a sparkling challenge. 'Why not?

You were very persuasive, and there has to be a first time for everyone. I suppose you could say you wore my resistance down.' She shrugged. 'It was a pleasant interlude, and I'm sorry if you feel under an obligation to me because of my inexperience!'

'Inexperience!' He echoed the word with a harsh laugh. 'Innocence is the better word. Dear God, Verona, how do you think I feel?'

'Somewhat chastened, I trust,' she rejoined smartly. 'And not before time, if you want my opinion. Perhaps your future judgements of unknown females will be more charitable.' He mustn't sense how near to collapse she was, how dearly she would have loved to have thrown herself into his arms and accepted his offer. He had been right. For her, marriage to him would be a challenge worthy to address herself to, and one she would willingly have embraced in any other circumstances than the ones in which she found herself.

'Will nothing change your mind?' he asked without emotion.

Miserably she shook her head as tears welled in her eyes, and a choking barrier formed in her throat. Andreas rose to his feet, having resumed the previously discarded trunks, to stand facing her, his countenance hard and set. Impulsively she placed a hand on his bare arm, feeling the skin flinch at her touch. For a brief second she closed her eyes, assimilating the shock that touching his body could still give her.

'I...' she began hesitantly. 'I'll never forget what happened tonight but—but it was wrong, Andreas, and it would be even more wrong if you felt obliged to act against your instincts by offering me marriage, to offset consequences that are never likely to happen.' She paused, more apprehensive of his lowering silence than any bitter words, then plunged on, 'In the circumstances, I think it best I return to England without further delay.' A surge of pain sliced through her heart as she heard the words leave her own lips, but really she had no alternative. The truth was, she should have left two weeks ago, before Andreas's plan of seduction had been put into operation. 'I'll leave a note for Katina saying I've been offered a job and can't afford to turn it down.'

'I see.' Any vague, illogical hope that he'd continue to argue with her faded as Andreas's dark head dipped in acquiescence. 'If that's your final decision then I'll book you a flight as soon as the airport office opens tomorrow.' His eyes, heavy and torpid, moved from her face to the horizon, where a slash of coral sky announced the birth of the morning. 'Today,' he corrected himself without emotion. 'Sleep well in your last few hours in Crete, *yatáki mou.*'

He brushed past her, re-entering the villa, leaving her alone to watch the needles of light pierce the morning sky. It was some time before she even realised her face was wet with tears.

Twelve hours later Verona watched Andreas manhandle her suitcase through the check-in. During the long daylight hours that had preceded her afternoon flight she'd thought he might make another attempt to get her to change her mind about leaving, but he'd remained aloofly silent. In fact, she thought heavily, he'd distanced himself so far from her that they could have been strangers. She wished they didn't have to part like this. Why couldn't Andreas see that she was doing him a favour by refusing his chivalrous offer? He had a warm, passionate nature that deserved to be nurtured by a woman he loved as well as desired. By leaving him she was truly showing the depth of her feelings for him—if he did but know it!

Unconsciously she squared her shoulders and thrust her small chin proudly aloft as he weaved his way back to her through the crowd milling around the small foyer of the airport.

'Have you got your passport ready?' He handed her the baggage check as he asked the question in a politely distant voice.

She nodded, a pulse in her throat racing fast now the final moment of parting had come.

'I'll write to Katina.' She kept her voice determinedly cheerful. Partings were always dreadful. She'd never forget how she'd felt when she'd waved her mother goodbye: the desolate feeling as she had passed through passport control to the departure lounge. Only this was worse by a hundredfold.

'I'll tell her.' Andreas's tone was as composed as his face, giving nothing away. 'Also, you should know I've spoken to my uncle Yorgos on the phone instructing him to pay you the salary we agreed—plus the bonus you've earned—in whatever form is most acceptable to you.'

'No!' Her eyes widened in horror. 'I don't want your money, Andreas. I only agreed at the beginning because I'd no idea what would happen. But Kati's my friend and I enjoyed being with her. I'm only too happy that Irini misunderstood what you intended . . .' She stopped, appalled, raising her hand to her mouth as she realised what she'd said.

'Ah—Irini!' It was an angry and triumphant interruption. 'So she did let something slip, after all. No wonder you regarded me as some kind of ogre. I must admit I wondered that night at the party. It didn't seem possible that Grafton knew enough to upset you so thoroughly. It was another reason why I decided to approach Kati without delay, in case she was hugging some indeterminate fear to her heart.'

'She was,' Verona admitted. 'And she was overjoyed to discover it was Stephanos who wanted her. I think she must have always been very fond of him.'

'That was my opinion, too.' He looked at her gravely. 'And I still believe it so, but I shall see they are betrothed a full twelve months in case she changes her mind. And as for the money—it's yours, Verona. It was a business arrangement for services rendered, and you earned it. I insist you accept it!'

It was cruelly said as Verona felt the blood drain from her face. It wasn't the way she'd wanted them to part. They'd been both friends and lovers; surely at least they could part as friends?

'Andreas...please...' Hazel eyes begged him. 'Please try to understand...' She laid a tentative hand on his arm, taken by surprise when he pulled her towards him, gathering her tightly, crushing her mouth with unrestrained passion. Deep within her a feeling of intense pleasure was born, spreading tentacles of fire through every limb. She found herself clinging to him, pressing herself against his strong body, torturing herself with this last sensual assault.

'Oh, I understand, *yatáki mou*.' The fierce whisper scorched her ear as he abandoned her mouth with a cruel suddenness, leaving her gasping, hungry for the taste of him. 'It was a sweet revenge you planned, and the fact that I deserved it makes it no less painful!'

'Revenge?' she breathed, not understanding.

'To make me believe that you loved me.' His breath came harshly as pain twisted across his face. 'You told me once you only gave your body to a man when he had your heart—and I believed you, my sweet. So what was I to think when I discovered I was the first man to know you, hmm?'

'Andreas...' she protested, feeling a little faint and still conscious of the throbbing tissue of her mouth. He was being grossly unfair. It was his love that was in question—not hers!

He ignored her interruption, gripping her shoulders and glowering down into her widened eyes with a steely stare. 'Enjoy your triumph, Verona, because you gave a valuable gift away to gain your retribution. I only hope you don't live to regret it. It's possible that when you do meet a man you can love as much as I loved you and he feels the same way about you, you may wish you hadn't wasted your innocence on a man you despised!'

'I don't despise you, Andreas!' Pale with shock, Verona seized on the last part of his sentence to deny it. But he'd said something else. Her fevered brain recalled his words. Andreas had said he had loved her, and it had sounded as if he'd meant it! She licked her dry lips, almost afraid to question him, but aware she couldn't go out of his life not knowing. 'You—you said you—you loved me?' she asked hesitantly.

'You want your last drop of blood, *yatáki*?' The acid in his tone was unmistakable, and his face was so close that she could see the little lines of strain at the corners of his mouth. 'It pleases you to pretend you didn't know how I felt about you? You want to hear it from my own lips before you go?'

Verona shivered at his uncompromising tone, averting her face from the cruel glitter of his eyes and trying to ignore the cold tremors glissading down her spine. 'How could I know?' she pleaded. 'You never spoke of love...'

'You are not blind, *agapi mou*. You can read what's in a man's heart when he looks at you. Do you really not know that when I lit the candle in Iraklion Cathedral it was a petition to Our Lady to awaken in *you* the feelings that were already possessing *me*? And on the boat, when I wanted you so desperately and I told you that I loved you, have you forgotten that...?'

But he hadn't, he hadn't! He had asked her if she wanted to hear him say the words and she'd told him 'no'. She'd thought he was acting a part, but now she was having doubts.

'I see you do remember,' he said tautly. 'Ah, Verona, you can laugh at me—I have no defence. I thought I'd fallen in love with a woman who could match me fire for fire. A beautiful woman who would stand by my side and face whatever challenge life should fling at the two of us.' He stared down at her, his face drawn. 'There is too much of my father in me to settle for beauty alone. I'd waited so long for a woman I could really love as well as desire, someone who would match me in mind and spirit as well as heart...and you were the one. I knew it long before we became lovers.'

'Yes, but...' She paused, confused. 'It was only after—after you discovered I'd never had another lover and thought I could be pregnant that you mentioned marriage...'

'Because your ambitions lay elsewhere—as you'd made only too clear. I didn't want to frighten you off. I hoped that after we were lovers I could persuade you to look at marriage in a more attractive light. That was my original plan.' He gave a bitter laugh. 'Then, when I discovered you'd saved your innocence against all the temptations you must have faced, I was arrogant and fool enough to imagine that, like me, you too had lost

your heart . . . that I was as special to you as you to me,
that you wanted to share the rest of your life with me—
that marriage was the obvious conclusion . . . until you
disillusioned me!'

Verona stood there transfixed, unable to utter a word.
If only he'd said these things to her last night—or earlier
today—instead of maintaining a brooding silence. Now
it was too late. Not only must his professed love for her
have withered in the face of what he saw as her wilful
deception, but there was no time to defend herself. Her
luggage was already on its way to the plane and their
intense altercation was already drawing attention from
interested bystanders.

'So you see, *mahtia mou*, you have achieved what you
doubtless set out to do—hurt me a hundred times more
deeply than the pain I inflicted so unjustly on you, and
who can blame you?' He bent his head and brushed his
mouth tantalisingly against her own in a kiss just brief
enough to leave her feeling hollow and hungry as he drew
away. 'Take the money I owe you, Verona; that was a
business contract. This is personal.' He eased a bulky
parcel from the jacket of his coat, and thrust in into her
hands. 'I hope when your ship comes home it brings you
everything you want. And now you'll forgive me if I
don't watch you walk through passport control. I find
prolonged goodbyes tedious!'

He rammed his hands into his trouser pockets, glared
down at her for a few brief seconds, then, before she
could find the will to speak, he had turned on his heel
and was striding away through the crowd, which parted
automatically before his purposeful progress, to disappear through the plate glass doors into the afternoon
sun without a backward glance.

It took a sharp bang on her shoulder to bring Verona back to her senses.

'Sorry, love.' A young Englishman tossed an apology over his shoulder as he forced his way round her towards passport control. She couldn't just stand here blocking the right of way—yet she wasn't prepared to take the last few steps that would take her into the no man's land of the departure lounge. Instead she made her way into the large restaurant opposite where she stood. Needing nothing, she bought a coffee to give herself an excuse to sit down at one of the tables.

Andreas had said he had loved her. It had been all she needed to know, but he hadn't waited for her explanation. Suppose she went after him and told him her fears, explained why she'd turned him down? Would he understand, or was the gulf between them too wide? Perhaps she should accept the situation as it stood: return home, get the job she wanted, take up her life anew. There would be other men... But none like Andreas Constanidou!

Almost unthinkingly she unwrapped the parcel he'd given her, gasping when the contents of its cushioned box revealed a lump of amethyst, the purple crystals cut jaggedly to represent a rough sea. Upon the sea there was a yacht of such intrinsic beauty that she stared, transfixed. The whole craft was made of gold. From the hull rose a slender mast from which two thin but solid sheets of gold had been formed into the mainsail and topsail. On the other side a spinnaker had been fashioned from thin golden wires, billowing out as if filled with the power of the *meltimi* itself. Wonderingly she turned it over in her hand, her breath catching in her throat as she read the inscription. It was in Greek, but now the alphabet presented no difficulty to her. Carefully she mouthed the words to herself—'Verona—s'agapo—Andreas.' S'agapo!—I love you!

How long had he had this in his possession? He must have bought it and had it engraved in Iraklion—long before they'd become lovers. Dear God, what was she doing here, even thinking of leaving Crete? Now she knew he really had loved her, there was only one place she could logically be! Somehow she would make him understand her own doubts and fears, and how they had vanished now she was sure of his love.

Grabbing up her hand luggage, she carefully placed the repacked box inside it and made for the exit.

Her breast heaving with excitement, she was soon outside in the hot, scented air. A glance at her watch told her she'd spent longer than she'd thought agonising in the airport restaurant. Her flight was at that very moment about to take off with at least one empty seat!

Unzipping her bag, she searched for her purse. She should have enough drachma to get her back to the villa, or—a thought struck her—would Andreas go back to the apartment in Iraklion? Katina was due back this evening, but she'd no idea to which address Stephanos would be returning her.

In consternation, she bit her lip.

'Do you need help at all? Is someone meeting you or are you trying to find a taxi?'

Verona started as the well-loved male voice spoke immediately behind her. Even before she turned, she knew the speaker would be Greek. The triple-aspirated 'h' in the word 'help' had betrayed what was otherwise a flawless accent.

She turned, her body vibrant with indescribable joy. He had waited for her! It was all the proof she needed to know she still had a place in his heart.

'Someone's meeting me.' Relief shone clearly on her face as she flung herself into Andreas's arms.

'I never gave up hope, *yatáki mou*,' he whispered as he gentled her face with his ardent kisses. 'I had to let you go, but I prayed you'd give me another chance to win your love. I was sitting here in the car, waiting for your flight to take off. Waiting until my last hope had faded before I could bear to drive away...and then I saw you...' His voice was gruff with emotion, as the heavy drone of jet engines drew their attention to the sky.

'Oh, Andreas...my luggage is on that! I've got no clothes!'

He threw back his head and laughed at her distress. 'In the circumstances, I'll buy what you need and I'll pay for them.' His face broke into a wicked grin. 'On this occasion I must insist your preferences take second place to my desire.'

Laughing up into his autocratic face, alive with love for her, Verona accepted her cue. 'Has there ever been a time when they didn't?'

His eyes bright with emotion, Andreas told her solemnly, 'That's something you must answer for yourself, *yatáki*.'

For a few moments she pretended to consider, her face flushed with happiness, her hair a golden curtain on her shoulders.

'Yes, Andreas,' she said at last, her voice throbbing with sincerity so he could read into her answer the fulfilment of his dreams. 'I confess there have been times when my preferences and your desires have met on common ground.'

Then, just in case he hadn't got her message straight, she locked her gaze into his own as she told him, 'I love you, Andreas, and I want to accept the challenge you offered me—if the position's still open.'

'It's open,' he assured her. 'Oh, yes, *yineka mou*, it's open!'

'Yineka?' She repeated the Greek word doubtfully, aware of its familiarity but in her dazed state of mind not immediately capable of translating it.

Andreas smiled his captivating smile straight into her puzzled eyes. 'My woman, my wife...' he interpreted softly, then prevented her from asking further questions by the simple expedient of sealing her lips with his own.

 *Harlequin Romance*

Coming Next Month

#3007 BLUEPRINT FOR LOVE Amanda Clark
Shannon West knows that renovating an old house means
uncovering its hidden strengths. When she meets Griff Marek,
an embittered architect—and former sports celebrity—she
learns that love can do the same thing.

#3008 HEART OF MARBLE Helena Dawson
Cressida knows it's risky taking a job sight unseen, but Sir Piers
Aylward's offer to help him open Clarewood Priory to the
public is too good to miss. Then she discovers that he wants
nothing to do with the planning—or with her.

#3009 TENDER OFFER Peggy Nicholson
Did Clay McCann really think he could cut a path through
Manhattan, seize her father's corporation—and her—without a
fight? Apparently he did! And Rikki wondered what had
happened to the Clay she'd idolized in her teens.

#3010 NO PLACE LIKE HOME Leigh Michaels
Just when Kaye's dreams are within reach—she's engaged to a
kind, gentle man who's wealthy enough to offer real security—
happy-go-lucky Brendan McKenna shows up, insisting that *he's*
the only man who can really bring her dreams to life....

#3011 TO STAY FOREVER Jessica Steele
Kendra travels to Greece without hesitation to answer her
cousin Faye's call for help. And Eugene, Faye's husband, seems
grateful. Not so his associate, Damon Niarkos, the most hateful
man Kendra's ever met. What right does he have to interfere?

#3012 RISE OF AN EAGLE Margaret Way
Morgan's grandfather Edward Hartland had always encouraged
the enmity between her and Tyson—yet in his will he divided
the Hartland empire between them. Enraged, Morgan tries to
convince Ty that he's a usurper in her home!

Available in October wherever paperback books are sold, or
through Harlequin Reader Service:

In the U.S.
901 Fuhrmann Blvd.
P.O. Box 1397
Buffalo, N.Y. 14240-1397

In Canada
P.O. Box 603
Fort Erie, Ontario
L2A 5X3

COMING IN OCTOBER

SWEET PROMISE

Erica made two serious mistakes in Mexico. One was taking Rafael de la Torres for a gigolo, the other was assuming that the scandal of marrying him would get her father's attention. Her father wasn't interested, and Erica ran home to Texas the next day, keeping her marriage a secret. She knew she'd have to find Rafael someday to get a divorce, but she didn't expect to run into him at a party— and she was amazed to discover that her ''gigolo'' was the head of a powerful family, and deeply in love with her....

Watch for this bestselling Janet Dailey favorite, coming in October from Harlequin.

JAN-PROM-1

Harlequin American Romance®

SUMMER.

The sun, the surf, the sand...

One relaxing month by the sea was all Zoe, Diana and Gracie ever expected from their four-week stays at Gull Cottage, the luxurious East Hampton mansion. They never thought they'd soon be sharing those long summer days—or hot summer nights—with a special man. They never thought that what they found at the beach would change their lives forever. But as Boris, Gull Cottage's resident mynah bird said: "Beware of summer romances...."

Join Zoe, Diana and Gracie for the summer of their lives. Don't miss the GULL COTTAGE trilogy in American Romance: #301 *Charmed Circle* by Robin Francis (July 1989), #305 *Mother Knows Best* by Barbara Bretton (August 1989) and #309 *Saving Grace* by Anne McAllister (September 1989).

GULL COTTAGE—because a month can be the start of forever...
